About the Author

   Robert J. Berens, a veteran of World War II, Korea, and Vietnam, spent thirty-two years in the United States Army, rising in rank from infantry recruit to colonel. Since retiring in 1977, he teaches written communications at college level and writes defense-related articles for professional magazines. Although Following Polaris is his first novel, he has published three books of nonfiction.

FOLLOWING POLARIS

A NOVEL BY ROBERT J. BERENS

TURNER PUBLISHING COMPANY

TURNER PUBLISHING COMPANY

Copyright © 2001 Col. Robert J. Berens

Publishing Rights: Turner Publishing Company

All Rights Reserved.

Written by Robert J. Berens

Graphics by Leslie K. Berens

Kristi Johnson, Editor

Dayna Spear Williams, Editor

Tyranny J. Bean, Designer

Library of Congress Catalog Number: 2001087359

ISBN: 978-1-68162-409-9

Events depicted in Following Polaris--a novel based on post-World War II ambiguities--are historically accurate. Characters are authentic; however, similarities to actual people are poetical and coincidental. -RJB

Additional copies may be purchased directly from the publisher.

TABLE OF CONTENTS

I heard the bullets whistle, and believe me, there is something charming in the sound.

—George Washington

CHAPTER I

NATIVE'S RETURN

Don Bauer held a riddle... deep within himself. He pondered its implications as he rode the crowded bus from Council Bluffs to Homesite, Iowa, on June 22, 1945. Why wasn't he prideful, exhilarated? Wasn't he returning from the war after four long years? Hadn't he survived the Mediterranean battlefields physically intact? And hadn't his side—the Allies—been victorious?

Popular lore held that he was a hero. And he had done it in the best American tradition – lying about his age and enlisting in the Army at age seventeen. Even the recruiter at the time knew Don wasn't being truthful, but the lad's act was considered patriotic in the aftermath of Pearl Harbor. The times called for heroes—any way they could be garnered. And now even Don Bauer—despite his ambivalence—had to admit he had been courageous... at times. That he had fought with the 34th Infantry Division (Red Bulls), which had the most continuous combat days of all American divisions, spoke eloquently of his wartime service, surely.

As he stared out the bus window, the telephone poles gliding past seemed shorter and closer together than he remembered. This observation did not surprise him: just about everything seemed different from his recollections of southwest Iowa years ago.

Don mused over changes he would find at the small farm one mile west of town. His parents would be older looking, of course, less hardy, mellower. His two sisters would be wholesome, more mature and wiser, surely. His two brothers, away in the military services, would be bigger, more confident and zestful when they eventually returned. Only Sparky, the feisty little mongrel, would be unchanged—if any sentimentality remained in this battered world.

He asked the driver to drop him off short of Homesite. Don wasn't ready to be welcomed back just yet; he preferred easing into the meetings and greetings that awaited the first Homesiter returning from World War II. That fighting still raged in the Pacific added to the drama and poignancy of Bauer's return, of course.

Other passengers stared as he wrestled the duffel bag from the rack and stepped off the bus. Some probably recognized him as one of the Bauer boys, but which one? Hometown boys looked different in uniform, and it had been a long time: Don had changed from an adolescent to an adult since they had seen him last.

Rain had fallen the night before, so Don occasionally slipped in the mud of the unpaved lane leading over the hill to his home. But, then, Don was accustomed to Army hiking in the mud, so he plodded ahead steadily with the heavy bag slung over his shoulder. At the highest point he paused to gaze across fields toward town.

The water tower, "Homesite" in huge block letters on its side, loomed over the houses and buildings below. The power plant's throbbing generator still spewed diesel exhaust into the clear atmosphere. A stream of trucks and automobiles rolled up and down Highway 64, which he had just arrived on. A freight train struggled from the station at the head of a mile-long string of boxcars. Everything appeared dynamic, purposeful now in the Midwest—in sharp contrast to the prevailing listlessness when Bauer had departed years ago.

Crops greened the fields. Horse-drawn cultivators moved up and down arrow-straight rows of corn. Here and there a tractor droned away. A few terraces, marked by distinctive contours, curved about the hills. Limp weeds at roadside indicated use of a new chemical "weed killer." Modernity had crept onto the farmlands even as war preoccupied the nation's scientists and laboratories.

When he reached the Bauer's driveway, a dog next door barked. This was an unfamiliar animal to Don, but it served its purpose well. Edith Dearborne peered out her kitchen window and spotted Don. She reached for the phone and spun the crank.

"Central," the operator announced.

"The Jasons, please," Mrs. Dearborne requested.

Central made the connection - and remained on the line to "gather local news."

"Judy, this is Edith. Guess what? Don next door just came home."

And so Homesite was alerted. In short order, everyone knew that the returning soldier aboard the bus this morning was Don Bauer – the first to come back whole, without maiming or mutilation.

From within the white clapboard house, Don picked up sounds of dinner. (Lunches were not served in the Midwest, only breakfasts, dinners and suppers in that order.) Don stepped inside the kitchen and made out three people around a table: his parents and a neighbor helping John Bauer put up alfalfa hay.

Sparky reacted first, barking and dashing from beneath the table. However, when he recognized the "stranger" as Don, the little dog rolled engagingly on the floor. As Don stooped to stroke Sparky, Mom fairly shouted, "It's Don! Thank God."

Chairs scraped the linoleum flooring as the trio arose to greet him. When his eyes had adjusted to the dim interior light, Don saw his mother had not changed much. She was still robust, although gray streaked her dark hair. Outwardly – despite her initial outburst – she was surprisingly calm, typically so.

Not true of her husband. John Bauer rushed to embrace his middle son, exclaiming, "One down, two to go!" Tears glistened his cheeks.

Don noted Dad had lost most of his hair and a good amount of weight as well. However, the shocker was that he had lost his teeth altogether. Clearly, the war had devastated Dad.

Tony Ambrose, the neighbor, extended a hand and said, "Welcome back, Don. It's been a long time."

Don was benumbed rather than emotional. Since he had not dared to believe that he would return – for three years he wouldn't even think about it – he had to readjust now. But again he wondered about his lack of elation. Why wasn't he joyful?

Mom hastened to set another place and when all were seated she said, "Let's thank God for Don's return and ask that He bring the others home as well."

She crossed herself in Catholic ritual and closed her eyes. Don sat quietly while others prayed. He realized then that some things had *not* changed. Praying had always been imperative at the Bauers, maybe because they had had few other appeals. His thoughts of the painfully drab 1930s revived bitterness even on this gala occasion.

The meal itself – roast beef, mashed potatoes, garden salad, bread and butter, and apple pie –was a stark reminder. Seldom had such provision been tabled at the Bauer home when he was growing up. Persisting hunger, especially at bedtime, was the usual case.

Winter seasons had been the worst. Staph infections brought on by lack of fresh fruits or vegetables were inevitable. Don had quit playing basketball his senior year of high school because of yellow jaundice. ("You aren't eating right, my boy," the town doctor had said accusingly.) Of course, this had been a devastating verdict, for Don had "lived" to play basketball in those days.

Those long-ago first meals in the Army now came to mind. When others had complained of "army food," Don had relished it. In fact, he literally grew up in that first year of military service, adding three inches in height and twenty-five pounds in weight to his still maturing frame.

When he noted others staring, Don said, " Excuse me. I drifted off."

They quickly reassured him; after all, newspaper articles and radio casts had warned families that returning veterans may behave oddly at first. Still, Don had detected a telling frown on Mom's brow.

"We heard you'd be back," she said. " But after so many rumors and disappointments we wouldn't believe it till you showed up."

"Remember, Don, how they canceled your furlough right after Pearl Harbor?" Dad asked. "That was bad, real bad." "But not as bad as that Kasserine thing," Mom interjected. "That was the worst."

"Yeah," Dad agreed. "After that we pretty much shut everything out. We had to. It's the only way we could get by. So, we just had Father Kirkman say masses for you boys and hoped for the best."

"You're here today because we put our trust in God," Mom added. "I said the Rosary twice a day for you boys and God heard me. Now I am going to keep on saying it to thank Him."

Tony Ambrose was a bit uncomfortable in the midst of all this intimacy, but he wouldn't have missed it. Tony had no sons of his own, so this homecoming was as close to such drama as he would come. Besides, Don's being the first back made it unique.

"It was rougher on you than on me," Don said as he mulled Mom's explanation for his safe return. What if she knew of his skepticism? Would she accept it? Could she?

Don's dilemma was that he had concluded while fighting in Tunisia that God had little time for soldiers. Therefore, Don no longer consciously prayed. Oh, he might find himself praying in a moment of panic – habits are hard to break! – but once the crisis passed, that was it.

Not that he was comfortable with his despairing; perhaps he was an ingrate. However, his faith had ebbed after Ray Porder took a spray of machine-gun bullets in the chest even as he beseeched

God for protection. Stunned, Don had watched Ray's eyes turn glassy and his countenance relax as "God called him home."

Ray was not a Catholic and Don thought of baptizing his friend conditionally – just in case. But he hadn't. Instead, Don clumsily straightened Ray's body and covered the boyish face with a steel helmet. Ray was the first friend Don had *watched* die – and the last! Although he saw others die, he never watched again. Thereafter a parade of acquaintances proceeded to pass through as numbers easily erased. That was how Don came to question God's concern for soldiers.

Again noting glances, Don snapped back to the present. Mom was about to ask something but was interrupted by the entrance of Jeanne, the youngest of the Bauer siblings. Jeanne bounded into the house and changed the subject and the mood.

"Everybody's talking about you, Don," she bubbled as she embraced him. "You're famous!"

"Oh, I'm sure they are."

"True, true, true!" his sister gushed. "I was so excited that I ran all the way home."

"I'm flattered," Don responded. And he was. They had always been close, maybe because Don had babysat Jeanne so much. Once Dad and Mom had returned from a church bazaar at midnight to find Don carrying six-month-old Jeanne "horseback" to sooth her teething pains.

"You've grown up," Don managed to say now.

"Well, I'm almost fourteen," she rejoined. "I was only nine when you left. Remember?"

But even at this light moment, he turned sullen. That Jeanne had run all the way home reminded Don that the Bauers still walked to and from Homesite. True, not having a car had encouraged exercise; however, frequently it brought on embarrassment. Basketball trips, for example.

Players were taken to out-of-town games by parents. However, the Bauers with no car could hardly participate in ride sharing. Then, too, seldom did Don have the quarter expected by others to help pay for gas. This sometimes rankled a driver, other players too. Taunts were not unusual, but Don would gut it out, considering ridicule a small price to pay for playing basketball. But, now those long ago barbs knotted Don Bauer's stomach once again.

"Hey you! Pay attention to me," Jeanne chided good-naturedly. "You seem to be off somewhere else. A girlfriend, I'll bet."

"Sorry," Don said sheepishly. "I'm still getting used to being here."

"It'll take a while," Dad said as he and Tony got up from the table. "We'll go finish the hay. Won't take long and then we'll be back."

A short while later, Jeanne announced she would return to town. Although Don could not envision what she and her friends were up to, he was pleased that she seemed to be popular. Then, too, Mom encouraged her to leave; Mom wanted to "get down to brass tacks" with her middle son.

"Were you wounded?" she asked when they were alone. "I know you'd never tell me."

"Not seriously."

"Are you sure?"

"You would've heard from the Army," Don reassured her. "I would've had no say in that."

"Is anything else wrong?"

"Like what?"

"Stress. Did it get to you?"

"Oh, there were times, of course. But that's all past now."

Don was not surprised; in fact, he had prepared himself for this discussion. Mental depression had been on Mom's mind for a long time. Hadn't her father done away with himself rather than submit to a leg amputation? Then, too, during the 1930s Mom had suffered a nervous breakdown. She had recovered but feared "it" ran in the family. His conversational lapses over the past half-hour had not alleviated her concerns, certainly. Perhaps "battle fatigue" was why Don had now returned ahead of others, even some who had gone off to war before him.

After reassuring her to the extent possible, Don said he would walk to the field for exercise. Mom thought that was a good idea, especially since she had to clean up the kitchen and fix the room upstairs for him.

With Sparky trotting alongside, Don arrived in time to see Dad and Tony load the last bales on the hayrack. After a few moments, Don decided to join in. He grabbed a bale and found himself struggling to wrestle the awkward load onto the rack. His straining did not go unnoticed. Although both Dad and Tony quickly assured Don that his farming know-how would soon return, they appeared to take satisfaction in his poor showing. After all, farm labor demanded skill and strength. Smarts too!

Don turned down an offer to ride back. Instead, he and Sparky walked to the nearby creek that cut through the rolling hills. He waxed nostalgic when he reached the gorge and saw a clear stream of water flowing below.

The Bauer boys used to dam the stream to create a pool of water about three feet deep. There they would swim and frolic naked on hot summer days. When it rained rushing waters quickly wiped out the dam, but they never resented the "disaster."

Rains in dust-bowl days were occasions to celebrate not deplore, for they broke the dry spells, cleared the air and alleviated prevailing pessimism. Moroseness had been the bane of the 1930s. Dad would sulk for weeks on end, not speaking to anyone. Ironically, he would break out of the mood with a tirade against one of the boys, usually Don because of his brashness.

In fact, one such set-to sparked Don's joining the Army to find a new life—and incidentally a new Dad of sorts. A dispute had started over a trivial matter but when neither would back down, Don threatened to "go sign up." Dad said, "Good! Bring me the papers." Don complied, of course, and Dad signed them—with a trembling hand. Both would reflect on this bitter resolution in years to come —many times.

As he and Sparky now ambled homeward, Don looked toward Homesite. What were they saying about him there? What were they asking? There would be curiosity for sure, and when he finally visited town there would be endless questions, mostly repetitive. Well, he would put it off until Sunday when he attended the obligatory mass with his parents. That would be soon enough.

Back at the house, Don learned that Mrs. Dearborne had been there in his behalf. The Chairman of Community Club had called, and, since the Bauers had no telephone, asked Edith Dearborne to relay an invitation for Don to speak at the next meeting. When Mom told him this, Don reflexively asked, "What do they want from me?"

He recognized at once that he had disappointed Mom. She informed him that this was an honor. Besides, she belonged to the club and members had always been good to her. So Don agreed to accompany Mom to the upcoming Thursday meeting.

Another message: His older sister Deborah had called the Dearbornes and asked them to relay that she would be out tomorrow. Deborah, living in Omaha, already had heard that he was back and

wanted to see him right away. Don was both pleased and curious –
and eager to learn how near she came to his expectations.

The next morning Deborah arrived well dressed and made up. She
had an easy-going personality and seemed self-assured, more so than
he had expected. In his absence, she had put herself through business
school where she polished off typing, shorthand and basic accounting.
She now worked for an Omaha firm and earned enough to live comfortably. With another girl she rented an apartment. Deborah still dated
her high school sweetheart, Paul Capers, and planned to marry him
when they had saved enough to start farming.

Despite her outward confidence, Don suspected she would always
be dealing with early scarring, as he would be. One difference, though.
Whereas she tended to accept things philosophically, he did not. Odd
that this was so, for it was Deborah who had acquainted him with
Polaris.

On a clear summer night back in 1929, the Bauer kids were playing outside when Deborah announced she could find Polaris. Don was
intrigued when she pointed out Big Dipper and then measured out
from the cup to North Star. "Its scientific name is 'Polaris,'" she explained, "and it always marks true north. A compass can be wrong but
not Polaris. It'll always keep you on the right path."

Don was impressed, so much so that he enlarged Polaris's benevo-
lence beyond geographic orientation. For example, if he was at a loss
in explaining why he had done something intuitively, he would say, "I
followed Polaris." Who could ever argue with that?

The practice carried over. In fact, when he now announced that he
would be attending college, Mom was skeptical. He explained a new
GI Bill would take care of tuition, books and money for incidentals.

"Why would they do that?" Mom wanted to know.

"Sort of a bonus," Don replied. "To help veterans get started again."

"Well, I hope it works for you," Mom, who considered this another oddity in his behavior, said. "But I know one thing for sure: you
don't get anything for nothing in this life. There's always strings at-
tached."

"Mom, I'm going to try something besides farming and Polaris
points this way. What else is there?"

There was nothing else, of course, so Mom dismissed further discussion with "you and your Polaris!"

Sunday's Mass was a blur to Don. At the start of the homily, Father

Kirkman returned the congregation to its knees to thank God for Don's safe return, and to beseech Him further. "Oh, Almighty God, hear our prayers," the pastor intoned. "Return our sons to their beloved families, for we have suffered their absence much too long. Ah-men."

At the church entrance after the service, Don became involved in a guessing game. One slightly familiar face after another would ask, "Do you remember me?" Or, "I'll bet you don't know who I am." Once in a while, Don guessed right, but not always. A notable change on the part of all was their general buoyancy. Life had clearly improved for them. Even those who had lost someone in the war now valiantly accepted the loss as a contribution to a just cause—and names were already being added to the war memorial in the park.

More awkward were the questions and comments from young males. They just knew the war was the biggest thing in their lifetimes, so all were eager to join the fray in the Pacific. "I hope it don't end too soon," they would say. "I want to have a shot at those Japs!" To them it was simple, dramatic, and heroic.

Had he once been that way too? Really?

On the appointed Thursday, Don and Mom walked to the banker's house for Community Club meeting. Mom proudly reacquainted him with her friends. Seeing she enjoyed this bit of the limelight, Don was glad that he had come with her. After refreshments, the hostess announced next month's meeting and reported on three ailing members. Then she introduced "our very own Sergeant Donny Bauer, who will tell us about the battlefields."

Don gave a chronological account of his experiences since leaving Homesite. Every ear listened and every eye watched. Mindful of those with absent sons, Don described what it was like in abstract terms. Of course, he couldn't give them what they wanted: news and reassurance on loved ones. But they understood sacrifices, noble endeavors, and that most servicemen would survive, so that was the message he imparted.

Afterwards, the hostess thanked him and all applauded.

"You did well, Don," Mom said on the way home as a way of thanking him.

After these two exposures to Homesiters, Don felt more comfortable. At Mom's suggestion, he and Dad walked to town the next evening to renew old acquaintances. "We'll go to Larse's," Dad said. "They always ask about you."

Larsen's Tavern (everybody called it "Larse's") was the town hangout. Most evenings "influentials and hangers-on" gathered there to exchange news and views over beer (legal) and mixed drinks (illegal). Occasionally a woman would be there, but for the most part Larse's was a man's place.

Don soon found beer after beer being shoved his way. Dad, who seldom imbibed, now partook wholeheartedly. He was flattered by the attention, and from atop a barstool he talked and laughed with the best of them. At one point he proclaimed that he was proud of his "fighting sons." No one disagreed with that, of course.

Don talked to fathers and brothers of those he had served with. All seemed genuinely happy that Don had made it back safely and they asked the obvious.

Most wanted to know about the battle of Kasserine Pass, which had decimated units from southwest Iowa and cast a pall that still prevailed. Again, Don answered by explaining that because he was off on a special mission in Northern Tunisia, he had escaped Rommel's thrust. They all appeared to understand and said he had been lucky to get away.

At one point, Mose Langdon, a World War I veteran, sidled up and slyly quipped, "*Voulez-vous couchez avec moi?*"

"I'm impressed," Don replied, "that you recall French propositions after so many years."

"Let me tell you, Don," Mose lamented, "I wouldn't take anything for my time in 'Pay-ree.' The greatest days of my life, believe me."

"I never got to Paris," Don reminded him.

"But you were in Rome! I'm sure it was the same."

"Probably so."

"You've got a rude awakening coming," Mose continued ruefully. "This town's deadly. Hell, I envied you guys over there."

"Mose," Don reminded him, "the years have dimmed your memory. You forget that people were getting shot and going off the deep end every day."

Mose reflected a moment... "Did you get in on the occupation?" he asked. "That's where it happened. For a bar of soap or pack of cigarettes you could get anything you wanted, and I mean *anything*!"

Abruptly, he shifted the topic, "Have you ever thought of joining the Legion?"

Don said he hadn't, but maybe he should.

"I'll get you in," Mose confided, making it sound as though joining might be difficult. "Drop by and I'll fix you up."

Dad, not used to beer, had had enough after an hour or so. As he and Don prepared to leave, Bill Perkins, a well-to-do farmer and habitual patron of Larse's, slipped Don a car key. "Take your dad home in my car," Perkins said. "You'll find sugar in the back seat. Take a bag in to your mother."

"Generous of you," Don replied, "but…."

"It's O.K.," Bill assured him. "Nobody's going to jail, leastwise you. Ha! Ha!"

Abruptly, the idea appealed to Don. "Why not?" he said with a nod to Bill Perkins.

Dad had reservations though. As he and Don headed out of town in Bill Perkins' Buick loaded with black market sugar, Dad said, "I hope we don't get caught. Why, we'd be responsible for the whole load, and we'd be ruined!"

"We won't get caught," Don reassured him. "A bag of sugar is small pickings in this game, I'll bet."

Don surmised this may have been the most illegal act Dad had ever committed. On the other hand, Bill Perkins probably black-marketed daily. Perkins had land, livestock and clout, so why would he suffer shortages? As Mom would say, "Them that's got, gets!"

Don watched Dad and sugar disappear into the house before heading back to town. He returned the key and thanked Bill Perkins but turned down "a real drink." Don preferred to end the evening at that point and state of intoxication. The stroll home that summer night under a star-filled sky was soothing indeed.

Funny, but he had forgotten just how clearly the stars could shine in Iowa. He looked northward, spotted Big Dipper. Taking the distance between Merak and Dubhe as measurement, he projected outward five times and picked up Polaris. "I'm indebted to Deborah for that little pearl," he mused aloud.

For the moment at least, he didn't envy Bill Perkins and all that he possessed. Perhaps Perkins drank so much because he had so little, really. Don, on the other hand, possessed nothing, but he had vision beyond Homesite, Iowa. Maybe, just maybe, things were on the upswing for the Bauers.

In the days following, Don saw signs of improvement elsewhere. Jeanne, was clearly a star. She was not only popular with peers but was also beloved by elders. She was at ease in social settings, a good dancer and even took piano lessons. She viewed nothing too seriously and expected everything to turn out favorably. Why not?

Then, too, Don came to appreciate the standing within the community of his younger brother, Brad, now with the Seabees in the South Pacific. As farmers would say, Brad had cut a "wide swath" during his high school years. Not only did he stand over six feet tall at age sixteen, but he also had all the attributes of a gifted athlete: speed, size and strength. Brad had taken the small parochial high school basketball team all the way to the state tournament in his junior year, 1943. Of course, Don, fighting Germans in North Africa, was unaware of his younger brother's prowess.

As he now listened to others praise Brad, Don drew a comparison to his own high school athletic fortunes. Standing a mere five feet eight inches tall and weighing 140 pounds at the time, Don not only battled competitors for a spot on the basketball team but mundane handicaps as well. After practice on cold fall nights, he would scoop the day's picking of corn into a crib rising four feet or so above his head. Early the next morning, Don would start the coal-burning stove before the others arose and then he headed to the barn to milk the cow before breakfast. In this way he compensated for not doing chores he missed because of basketball.

"You have to hold up your end," Dad had rationalized. "Fair is fair."

Nor was there money for basketball trips or athletic equipment. However, Don managed to find gym shoes and a jock strap, both of which were ill fitting. During summers he eked out small sums by mowing lawns, pulling mustard weeds in grain fields and selling junk. Once he piled up all the scrap iron and steel he could lug home and received two dollars for his efforts from a local dealer who sold the scrap in Council Bluffs for much more.

Given the challenges, Don tended to believe almost everyone wanted him to quit basketball—to fail at the one big interest in his life. But he had a crucial ally—the coach.

Father Conway, the young assistant pastor who was short on basketball savvy but long on human compassion, encouraged Don unflinchingly. Thus, he improved steadily, playing a hard-charging game that usually caught up the whole team. Consequently, in three years the team went from a chronic loser to a consistent win-

ner. Don made the all-tournament team and was named team most valuable player in his senior year—despite a bout with yellow jaundice.

That Dad and Mom never attended a single game Don played had been a sore point; in fact, still was! When he received modest acclaim in his senior year, his parents seemed embarrassed by his success—even a bit apologetic. Not so with Brad a year later, however.

In an abrupt switch, Mom and Dad embraced Brad's participation in sports. Not only did they buy what he needed, but also they attended every game without fail. Dad especially basked in the exploits of his youngest son, going to town the morning after a big game to hear others recount Brad's starring role. Brad added to his own legend by quitting school after the 1944 basketball season and joining the Navy. He, too, wanted a hand in the biggest game of all—World War II.

Without a doubt, Don's leaving home under emotionally strained circumstances had contributed to Mom and Dad's reevaluation of their approach to child rearing. That something positive had resulted from his painful departure tended to ease Don's lingering bitterness at this late date.

Don began accepting past slights the morning after the night at Larse's. When he awoke, he spotted a footlocker in a corner of the room. It was the container he had used to ship home personal belongings before sailing to Europe in January 1942. He lifted the lid to find a clutter of letters, snapshots, trinkets, and a notebook. Anything of value had disappeared long ago. The fact that it had been rifled by his family in his absence was a reminder of how bad things had been back then. Don gently closed the lid and decided not to mention what he had come upon.

Not all revelations were painful, however. At breakfast Mom told Don he had a savings account. From his earliest days in the army he had sent home a monthly allotment from meager pay ($21 a month initially) to help out. He assumed the money had been spent, but now he learned that Mom had deposited some in a savings account.

"I started putting it away when you wrote us," she explained.

Apparently during a hiatus in correspondence while he was in Tunisia, Mom had given up, but when she heard again from him she decided he just might make it back. Of course, finances had been improving for the Bauers as well: Crops were bountiful and prices were up. In the little booklet she now handed him, Don noted a balance of over $2,000. That, along with his army separation allowance, would enable him to start college comfortably.

Don received another surprise through the mail that same day. A Selective Service notice stated he was delinquent in registering for the draft. He was now requested to report without delay to straighten out the matter.

The next morning he hitchhiked to the Selective Service Office in the County Courthouse some sixteen miles away. There were few cars on the highway, but he was confident someone would come along eventually. A highway patrolman happened by first and pulled to roadside near him. When Don approached, the patrolman asked for Don's Selective Service Registration Form.

"I'm just on my way to register now," Don replied.

"How old are you?"

"Twenty-one."

"A little late, aren't you?"

Don handed over the notice and his discharge papers, bemused at the irony of it all.

Now satisfied, the patrolman said. "Hop in, I'll give you a lift."

The officer talked readily once they were underway. He said he had tried to enlist in the Marines, but his eyesight was not good enough. Of course, it was good enough to be in law enforcement. Ha! Ha!

"I wanted the Marines cause they get the toughest fighting," he explained. "That's what I like, the toughest jobs."

Don let the patrolman talk on, a small price to pay for the ride.

"How about you?" the patrolman asked. "Who were you with?"

"The Army. I was in the Army over four years."

"Did you see action?"

"Some."

"Where?"

"Africa and Italy."

"Well, you're lucky! The Germans and Italians are like us. Now take those Japs, though. They aren't human. The Marines have to kill every one of them. Smoke them out with napalm and then kill them. That's why I wanted to join the Marines, to kill Japs."

"Soldiers burn them, too," Don reminded the patrolman.

"Yeah, but not like Marines. Actually, the Army just helps out the Marines most of the time. Even MacArthur picks the Marines for the toughest jobs."

When Don was let out at the Courthouse, the patrolman said, "I enjoyed talking to you. Good luck, buddy!"

"Thanks. And good luck yourself."

Don settled the matter with Selective Service within minutes. The clerk checked Don's discharge papers, updated the records, and returned with a completed registration form. He apologized for the inconvenience, but records had to be kept up. Don had learned he was not eligible for the draft since he was a discharged veteran.

A few days later, another discharged veteran showed up at the Bauer farm. It was Don's older brother, Frank, who had completed his missions as a B-24 tail gunner in the Eighth Air Force flying out of England. With the European war now over, B-24s were being phased out and their crews discharged. The vast distances in the Pacific required the new B-29 bombers to strike Japan. Then, too, high-level planners were aware of *something* that no one else even suspected.

Frank was highly elated. Not only was he out of military service but he had just become engaged to a girl from Missouri he had met while in training at Camp Leonard Wood. They planned on marrying as soon as things came together for them. Frank believed he could work out something with Dad and take over the Bauer farm.

"Dad's health isn't what it used to be," Frank confided. "Now he should ease into retirement."

"I'm not sure two families can make a living on such a small farm," Don cautioned.

"Maybe not," Frank replied. "But after what I've been through, I just want to get started at something."

"Do you need money?" Don asked.

"Do I! If money was toilet paper I couldn't wipe my tail. Elsie and me want to get married right away, but we're going to have to scrape like hell to do it."

"I'll lend you five hundred, if it'll help."

"Boy, would it ever! Rest assured I'll pay you back!"

Don took the money out of his newly found savings account, telling the banker he needed it for college. "Just consider it a wedding gift," Don told Frank, who again vowed he would pay it back as soon as he could.

The next day, Don rode the bus with Frank as far as Council Bluffs. Frank continued on to Missouri and Don walked to Mercy Hospital. There he asked a receptionist to page Joan Shea, a former high school friend now in nurse's training.

Joan had been a couple years behind Don, but they had socialized a bit while in high school. For a time after he entered the Army, they had corresponded regularly and signed off letters with "love." Over time, the exchange tailed off, however. Then during the time Don was out of touch correspondence stopped altogether. That was the "bad time," of course, when Don purposefully lost contact with everyone close.

Although this visit was unannounced, Joan came right down. She seemed thrilled to see him. He noted she had matured into a pretty young lady and was obviously bright as well. When he asked if she could get away for a while, she went to her supervisor. "I have an hour," she said upon returning.

They walked to a nearby coffee shop where they discussed many things, including the war. He explained why he had stopped writing and she said she understood, or thought she did.

"I'll better understand what you're talking about once I join up," she said.

"I hope it's over before you graduate, Joan. You don't need any of that."

She seemed disappointed by his comment. He studied her fair complexion, soft wavy blonde hair and wide blue eyes for a long moment. Incredibly, this lovely woman also wanted a shot at the Japs. She, too, wanted to be a part of this war that had already changed everyone's life.

While walking back to the hospital, they passed an empty garage bordering the sidewalk. On impulse, Don led Joan inside and they kissed, the first time ever! At the hospital doorway, she said she would let him know the next time she had a free weekend. Perhaps they could get together then. He said he would like that.

Over the next two weeks he helped neighbors with farm work, especially those who had been good to Dad. Sometimes Don was paid, sometimes he wasn't. Although he didn't care for farm work, he enjoyed those involved. Good-natured, patriotic and nonjudgmental, farmers were the best part of farming by far.

A stark announcement on August 6th portended war's end. An atomic bomb that "harnessed the power of the sun" wiped out Hiroshima, Japan, within minutes. (This was the *something* high-level planners had been aware of.) For several days the official reaction from the Japanese Government was silence, but Don doubted that even fanatics could withstand such devastation for long. Three days later a second atomic bomb struck Nagasaki.

CHAPTER II

WAYWARD BEARINGS

On August 13th, Don caught a bus for Iowa City and the University of Iowa. He arrived at the college town that evening and walked about the campus. Old Capitol stood at the center and from its steps Don looked westward to the Iowa River flowing serenely below. The scene was everything he expected a college campus to be.

He stayed at the Jefferson Hotel that night. Early the next morning, he had breakfast at a small restaurant nearby. Then he walked around to locate bookstores, clothing stores, and eating establishments. When the Registrar's Office opened at eight o'clock, he was there.

"I'm a veteran and I want to enroll in engineering," he told the receptionist, half expecting her to turn him around and send him on his way. Instead, she was courteous and cooperative.

"You'll want to see Dr. Cotter," she said and left the room.

Shortly, a tall avuncular man entered with right hand extended. "Welcome, my boy," he said. "I'm Dr. William Cotter, head of the Veterans Office on campus. You are the second veteran so far, but I'm expecting many more."

After expressing gratitude for all that Don had done for country and university, Dr. Cotter personally led Don through registration. In less than an hour he was enrolled as a college student. Dr. Cotter told him classes would begin in about three weeks, bid Don goodbye, and extended an invitation for him to return any time. Don was surprised at how simple it had been.

On his way back to the hotel, Don had second thoughts. Everyone seemed more confident of his ability than appeared warranted. He had been accepted in engineering with a sketchy math and physical science background, not to mention he had not been in a classroom for five years. Perhaps he needed advice from educated Homesiters; surely, the dentist, pharmacist, or school principal could counsel him. Feeling somewhat relieved, he caught a bus for home in late afternoon.

The trip started in unremarkable fashion, but when they reached Grinnell at about seven-thirty p.m., crowds were gathering and people were shouting and carrying on. At a stoplight, the driver asked a passerby what was going on.

"Truman just announced the Japs have surrendered!" was the reply.

Celebrations were occurring in every town and city along the way. Fireworks, dancing in the streets, hugging and kissing, and spontaneous cheering were rampant as Don's bus rolled westward. Don was ambivalent as he observed wild celebrants in town after town. What he welcomed, really, were long stretches of open highway free of din and tumult. He fell asleep after a while, having closed out all thoughts of World War II.

A festive mood prevailed that fall, however, as veterans returned in a steady stream. Everyone had catching up to do. Romances and courtships blossomed in the midst of reinvigorated social events. Dancing was the rage at the time and big bands flourished to play fast numbers for jitterbuggers and slow rhythms for romantics.

Inevitably, betrothals and marriages followed. Homesiters were breathless at the pace and vagaries of wooings and pairings. The Bauer family kept apace. Frank and Elsie were married that fall down in Missouri, and Deborah and Paul announced their engagement with a probable wedding date next year. But not everyone had matrimony in mind.

In late August, Don bumped into Bernie Schroeder, who had been Don's best friend back in high school. Bernie had just been discharged from the Air Corps and was interested in going to college. After a bit of good-natured bantering, Bernie got to the point, "I'm going into the Catholic priesthood," he announced. Bernie had decided this while flying bombing missions over Germany in a B-24.

Don was shocked. Bernie had been one of the orneriest guys in high school, having done everything at least once! When Don so reminded him, Bernie's response was simply, "God changed me."

Don's skepticism persisted: "You know, Bernie, we all had moments when we'd do just about anything to make it back, promise God anything! Sure that's not what happened to you?"

"This is different. Actually, I was wondering if you'd be considering the same thing. Remember we took Latin together back in high school? God was telling us something, Don."

"Not me! I took Latin because I couldn't afford typing. I suffered through four years of Latin because I had no choice."

"But what about that letter when you were in combat? That really impressed me."

"That letter was after I'd just seen my best buddy die and I needed to sort things out. I got a lot off my chest in that letter."

"And what did you decide?"

"You're not going to like this, Bernie, but I put all that behind me."

"You gave up on God?"

"You could say that."

"And now?"

"Oh, I go through the motions."

"But, Don, you came back! God answered your prayers!"

"Somebody else's, maybe," Don explained. "Mom was praying for me. But what about Ray Porder? He prayed to see his son, but he didn't make it."

"God had a purpose, Don."

Don smiled wryly and quipped, "Everything for a purpose! He makes billions of stars follow strict orbits, yet allows humans to be so confused and disordered."

"He gave us free will, Don, to test us!"

"It still makes no sense, Bernie."

Uncomfortable with his friend's skepticism, Bernie asked about Ray Porder.

"You'd of liked him," Don replied. "He'd do crazy things."

"Such as?"

"He 'knocked up' a girl and joined the Army to beat the rap. He was only eighteen at the time, even his parents urged him to skip out. But Ray went back and married the girl, after all. Boy, did we razz him!"

"He felt responsible," Bernie rationalized, "God doesn't expect us to be perfect. He just wants us to act responsibly."

Don ignored the philosophy and continued: "Ray never saw his baby. We went overseas and he was locked in for the duration. And how!"

"That seems tragic all right."

"Then his wife kept writing me. Pathetic letters. She'd ask if Ray was really dead, and if Ray really loved her. I wrote back a couple times, tried to get around the censor, but I quit after a while."

"I can understand that."

"And I stopped writing everyone else, too."

"Now that I can't understand!"

"Oh, I sent a couple of those GI telegrams that just said, 'Am O.K. Love, Don.'"

"But God did take care of you, Don."

"Mom agrees."

"Tell me, were you more reckless after your friend was killed?" Bernie asked.

"Not really reckless, but I'd do what I had to do."

Sensing there was more, Bernie waited.

"Like shoot a prisoner." Don volunteered.

"You shot a prisoner of war?"

"When I was told to. Once we had a couple Germans and we had to bail out. Lieutenant said, 'Shoot 'em'. I shot one and another guy shot the other."

"I couldn't have done that, shoot someone in cold blood."

"I said 'this one's for Ray' and pulled the trigger. It wasn't difficult."

"Of course you had little time to think about it under the circumstances?" Bernie reflected. " Maybe I was lucky, when my plane dropped bombs I couldn't see what happened."

"Well, you didn't hit what you thought you did. A lot of women and kids got blown to bits along with those ammunition factories, Bernie. Yeah, you were lucky. Maybe that's why the war defined us differently. I saw it up close, you didn't."

Bernie still maintained Don wasn't seeing the whole picture, God's Divine Plan. Thus, Don was despairing. "I'll pray for you," he promised.

"You do that, Bernie."

Shortly thereafter, Don received a note from an ex-army friend, Speck Mitchell. Speck, too, had just been discharged and invited Don to Benson, Iowa, where he had opened a beer hall. Speck's explanation typified the man who had "taken Don to raise in the Army": "Since I can't stop drinking, I got in the liquor business so that I'll save money, make a profit, and get drunk all at the same time."

Don asked a mutual acquaintance, John Bronson, to drive him to see Speck. They went on a Sunday afternoon and easily found "Speck's Place" in the small town. However, the building was locked because of blue laws, so Don knocked on the door of a little house nearby. Shortly, a stocky, balding man in his mid-forties opened the door.

"Well, I'll be damned if it ain't ol' Don hisself!" Speck exclaimed.Don grasped the proffered hand and said, "Good to see you. I was afraid my 'old Dad' wouldn't make it back!"

"You were, huh? Well, no damned Kraut was going to do in this rugged Irishman!"

"How're you doing, Speck?" Bronson asked when Speck noticed him.

"Everybody once and some twice," was the quick retort. "Let me get my shoes on and we'll go next door. This calls for a celebration!"

When Speck returned, the trio walked to the rear of the beer hall.

"I can't open Sundays," Speck explained, "but we'll sit out back and have a beer."

Already he was sweating profusely, an indication that he had been drinking heavily the night before. With his right hand, Speck wiped the sweat from his brow and flicked the perspiration away, a habit Don recognized all too well from bygone days.

Speck unlocked the rear door and they entered a still smoky, elongated room. From a cooler he took out three bottles of beer, handing one to each of his guests. Then they went to the stoop outside.

"Let's see," Don reminisced, "you must be about forty-five."

"You remember?"

"How could I forget! Your birthday's the same as Dad's and you were born in 1900."

"Yep, and you're the same age as my boy, Duane."

Speck turned to Bronson and explained, "Don was the greenest kid I ever saw when he came to my tent. He didn't even have whiskers! I took him under my wing and brought him around pretty good. Then, like a damned fool, he volunteered for commando training in Scotland. I thought I'd seen the last of him then."

Turning to Don with an impish grin, Speck asked, "You still a virgin?"

"And I don't shave yet either," Don parried.

"You know, John, every payday I tried to take Don to a whorehouse so's he could learn about women. But he'd always say, 'not this time, Speck.'"

"I just didn't believe in fornicating," Don countered.

"Yeah, you know what they say about that," Speck said with a twinkle in his eye. "It's terrible – unless you're in on it!"

Speck paused while they laughed, then continued, "The closest I came to getting Don screwed was in New York City, but I got drunk and passed out."

"Yep," Don added, "Speck lost it all outside Dempsey's bar."

"Wasn't my fault," Speck said. "Them New Yorkers were so damned patriotic I just couldn't turn 'em down. I never spent a cent!"

"Patriotic hell! They were scared to death!" Don explained.

"Anyway, Don hauled me back to Fort Dix that night when I was drunk as a skunk."

"I shoulda had a medal!"

"And then on the train I accidentally said 'horseshit' in front of a lady and teed Don off. He got up and left. When the train got to Newark, I ran the other way and got off up front. Then the train pulled out and Don thought he'd lost me for sure. Boy was he sorry."

"Naw, Speck, I thought I was finally rid of you, and good riddance!"

"Anyway, I hid behind a post till he came by. Boy was he glad to see me!"

"And after all that, John, Speck missed formation the next morning!"

"Yeah, I was hung over and almost got busted."

"You see, John, Speck had no pride at all," Don chided. "He'd even drink with officers!"

"Don's still upset 'cause he had to walk back to camp once while I caught a ride in a jeep." Speck explained impishly.

"We were marching back from the range in the rain," Don added, "when Captain Hinson pulled alongside and said, 'Hop in, Sergeant Mitchell. We wouldn't want them maps to get wet, now would we?' They went back to Hinson's tent and got drunk while the rest of us slogged back soaking wet."

"You can hardly blame Speck," Bronson ventured. "Hell, I envy him!"

"Don never met good people 'cause he wouldn't drink," Speck said "He was prejudiced, that's what he was."

"If I'd gotten drunk, Speck would've kicked my ass," Don rejoined.

"Yeah, that reminds me" Speck said, "You owe me for bringing you up in the army."

"God yes!" Don agreed, "Speck hounded me more than my own folks had. And here I'd joined the Army to get away from that!"

"You were too hard on 'em," Speck cautioned. "You were a lot like Duane, who was giving me fits at the time. But John, I learned something from raisin' Don. It helped me understand my own son better."

They were interrupted when a curious Bensonite sauntered up to see what was going on. Soon others came by as well. By mid-afternoon, nine men had gathered – and complicated Speck's bookkeeping! As he served up beer after beer, Speck tried to keep tabs on a beer carton. It was a hit-or-miss effort, though.

When the cooler ran dry and the party broke up, Speck began announcing what each guest owed.

"Gee, thanks, Speck," the first one quipped. "I'll see you later."

"Thanks, hell!" Speck shot back. "Thanks and a nickel will fetch a cup of coffee but not a bottle of beer. Now, you come by tomorrow and pay up 'cause I got it written down, you hear?"

"Don't hold your breath, Speck."

"Reminds me of those weekend parties back in camp," Don said when the others had left. "I'll bet you never collected back then either."

"Trouble is I lose track and trust the 'honor' system," Speck lamented. "But there's no honor among drunks!"

Don explained to Bronson how every Friday during training, Speck would ice down a tub of beer and hide it under his cot. After Saturday inspection, Speck would pull out the tub and throw a poker party.

"Yeah, the cheap bastards would come by, win my money, drink my beer and leave me with a Sunday hangover."

"You had a lot of friends, though!" Don reminded Speck.

"With friends like that who needs enemies!" Speck rejoined, but he was pleased by Don's remark nonetheless.

When Don and John got up to leave, Speck thanked them for coming by.

"You too Speck," Don replied. "By the way, I forgot my billfold."

"Yeah, I know! John, Don's so tight he squeezes a nickel till the buffalo shits!"

"Hey! No tales out of school!"

"O.K. The beer's on me," Speck said. "I'd just as well be generous 'cause you're never going to pay anyway."

They drove away as Speck waved goodbye from the sidewalk.

"He is the most genuine guy I have ever known" Don said in the car. "Back in training, guys were always coming to Speck for help. Sometimes it was money, sometimes advice. So, living in Speck's tent was a real education. One night I was dropping off to sleep when a guy came up and whispered through the screen. The conversation went like this:

"Speck!"

"Yeah?"

"It's me, Mel James."

"Yeah, Jamesy, watcha want?"

"I think I got the clap'"

"Well, come in here and let's have a look."

(Speck shined a flashlight as James milked it down.)

"Yep, that's it Jamesy, heh, heh," Speck announced. "You got it all right! Better get yourself to a doc before it goes too far up."

"But that's not all, Speck."

"What else?"

"Well, I just got back off leave, so maybe I exposed my girlfriend, too."

"How's that?"

"The first night home, I went to a whore because my girlfriend had the rag on. That's where I got the clap – I think."

"Oh boy!" Speck exclaimed.

"What'll I do now?"

"Speck ventured that perhaps the girlfriend wasn't clean either, so maybe James should wait a while before declaring himself." Don concluded.

"Yeah, Speck's always real helpful all right," Bronson agreed. "Even though he had big problems at home. Divorce and wild kids."

"I know, but nothing ever seemed to get Speck down. Sometimes I think that's why he drinks so much though." Don concluded.

"Maybe. Remember he said you helped him understand his own kid better?" John asked.

"Yeah, that's pretty ironic because I couldn't get along with my own Dad either."

"Life's funny."

"Sure is."

Don cut short his summer stay at Homesite when he read in the

Omaha World Herald that Iowa Hawkeyes were welcoming "walk-ons" at football practice. He decided to give it a try, so he moved to Iowa City at the end of August and went to the Athletic Department where he was well received.

Although Don had not played football in high school, he had played in the Army. A coach who had lettered at Michigan State once encouraged Don to play college football after the war. "You're fast enough," he had said, "and you're competitive. Build up your bulk, though."

"Well, now, I'll see if he knew what he was talking about," Don muttered to himself.

Don Bauer went to Iowa City with another aspiration as well. Since social mingling usually involved dancing, he wanted to be good at it. His handicap was that he had been away when he naturally would have learned along with his peers. Now, they all were better dancers than Don, at least in his mind they were.

Bernie Schroeder was a case in point. He had remained in Homesite the first two years of the war and had learned to cut a rug with the best of them. Girls all loved to dance with Bernie now, because he showed them off well. Don, on the other hand, was a letdown to girls who weren't interested in teaching at that stage. Somewhere on campus there would be dance teachers, surely.

He never got around to discussing academics with educated Homesiters, however. So Don Bauer embarked on his college venture with little idea of what he was getting into; however, he knew what he was leaving behind. Nothing much, really! He would take his chances in Iowa City with a GI Bill and a determination to succeed. He was willing to try just about anything!

CHAPTER III

SORTING THROUGH

Don Bauer found hospitality in Iowa City: pleasant people, appealing accommodations and an encouraging setting. He was housed temporarily in a war-vacated fraternity house on Dubuque Street until men's dormitories could be reclaimed from Navy V-12 students. His housemates were mostly eighteen-year-olds fresh from high school, but there were a few veterans, too. The proctor was a graduate student and an army veteran.

The proctor asked Don if he would object to having Tatsuo Osaka, a Japanese descendent, for a roommate. Upon learning that Tatsuo was a Nisei veteran of World War II, Don was enthused; he had fought alongside Nisei soldiers in Italy and had utmost respect for them.

Tatsuo was quiet, considerate, but somewhat intimidating as a student. Obviously, he was bright and dedicated, since he was already hitting the books in his quest to become a dentist. When Don mentioned that he was out for football, Tatsuo smiled dismissively and said, "I'm too small for such games. Besides, I'm too busy. I plan to marry next year, so I must become a professional of some sort."

"Another guy with his life in order," Don mused aloud. "I envy you."

At the first football session, the equipment manager treated Don as though he were a star! Everything had to fit properly, so the aide adjusted pads, straps and garments. Don found this annoying; he'd always played with hand-me-downs before.

Don wanted to play halfback, but the coach assigned him to defensive cornerback; players had to handle both defense and offense in those days. Eagerly, Don tried to intercept every pass in his direction.

"Just knock it down, make sure!" the coach advised. "Sometimes that's better than an interception."

Don was flattered by the coach's attention. He vividly recalled the glory days of the Hawkeye Iron Men in 1939 and 1940, when they were nationally ranked and victors over Notre Dame. Of course, this 1945 team was a far cry from those stalwarts of the pre-war era; however, Coach Clem Crowe – an ex-Notre Damer – wanted to take the first step in getting back to those heady times.

Don was still on the squad when classes began. That practice cut into class work was not immediately apparent. In the meantime, he was saving the cost of the biggest meal of the day by eating supper at the training table. He wore – as did most players – the liner socks, T-shirts, and sweatshirts to classes, saving on clothing and laundry costs. Then, too, he enjoyed comradery of the players. Although most were better players than Don, they respected his maturity and competitiveness.

In class work, Don managed to keep up in Written Communications, History, and Sociology; however, he fell behind in Math and finally followed the instructor's advice and dropped back into remedial Algebra for no credit. Chemistry, too, revealed his scanty background, and he began skipping classes. His football-shortened days did not leave much time for tutoring.

When Don did not make the varsity roster, he considered dropping football. But he didn't because he became more encouraged with each practice. At times he even ran plays in the varsity backfield. As a reward for his persistence, Don made the trip to the Nebraska game at Lincoln. Because the Hawkeyes were behind in the fourth quarter, he got in for two running plays. The Hawkeyes lost 13-6 and ended the season with a 2-7 record. Don was invited out for spring practice where he could make a bid next year.

With football finished in November, Don soon grew restless from too little physical activity. He tried studying more, but time spent was not productive. He took a job working for two meals a day at Morrie's Diner. He first tried waiting tables, but when his awkwardness discomfited patrons he settled for dishwashing. The two hours passed quickly in the kitchen where he and fellow student workers could banter about out of sight.

His final grades for the semester were an A in History, C in Sociology, Satisfactory in Written Communications and remedial Algebra, and an F in Chemistry. He took heart in that he could do some things well, but realized that engineering was not for him. He switched to Liberal Arts at the beginning of the second semester and vowed to get on top of his subjects and stay there. He would decide on a major later.

He started well enough but learned of a February Golden Gloves Tournament to be held in Iowa City. Needing an incentive to work out, Don decided to enter. He began running three miles each morning on the university track regardless of the weather and punching the light and heavy bags in the Field House. He wore heavy shoes and timed himself to three-minute rounds throughout the daily drills. Since he had no one to spar with, he could only make believe by shadow boxing.

While in the Army, Don had boxed at every "smoker" that came up. He had grown from a lightweight to a middleweight and always managed to hold his own. He was nimble afoot, had a good left jab and a solid left hook. He had a suspect right hand, though. A tiny shell fragment from combat in Italy was still embedded in his right wrist, restricting motion and taking the snap out of his punch. If he hit too hard and too often with his right on the heavy bag he endured dull pain afterwards. Punching the light bag did not bother as much, however.

Despite a lack of sparring, Don was confident. His competitors now were Navy V-12 cadets and Don believed they would not be as tough as former army opponents. But then he thought he might have miscalculated upon meeting his first opponent in the ring. The sailor was reminiscent of a pro who had trounced Don in Italy in 1944. The flat nose, stocky build, and overall toughness were all there. Don's adrenaline surged, however, and he decided to "get him quick."

A step out of his corner before the bell rang, Don rushed across the ring. His opponent was surprised and covered up instinctively. Don smashed a left hook around the sailor's guard and sent him slumping to the floor. The crowd roared approval of this furious attack by a local fighter.

The sailor rose to a knee, shaking his head. He waited for the count to reach eight before standing. The referee dusted gloves and then waved the fight to continue. Don brushed off attempts to tie him up again and connected with a left hook, sending his opponent down once more. The referee stopped the fight, despite objections from both the sailor and his coach.

Some eight hundred fans cheered wildly. Don had established himself as a local hero having knocked out the pre-tournament favorite in less than a minute of fighting. Both Iowa City newspa-

pers carried pictures and wrote up his sensational victory in glowing terms the following day.

Another Iowa Citian, Don Gotti, also won by a knockout in the welterweight division. The boy's father, Bob, approached Don Bauer in the dressing room afterwards and offered to train him along with his son. "The two of you will help each other," he said. Bauer said he would consider the offer.

Don managed to win the middleweight title, but not so handily as in the first fight. His second opponent stayed away and was content to just finish the fight, so Don left-jabbed his way to a unanimous decision. In his second fight of the evening, Don fought a more determined sailor. Midway through the second round, they butted heads and Don sustained a gash at his hairline. Blood flowed in a steady trickle for the remainder of the match, while the Navy coach called repeatedly for the referee to stop the fight. Again, Don was awarded a unanimous decision. The tournament doctor stitched up the wound in the dressing room and told Don not to fight again until cleared by a doctor.

The Navy coach came by to congratulate Don and to make an offer. "I'll be back at Wisconsin coaching boxing this fall," he said. "I may have a spot for you." When Don asked if there would be financial assistance, the coach said, "I'll let you know after I get on board, so keep in touch."

A local reporter did a feature on Don's prowess and wondered why the university didn't have a boxing team. Paradoxically, the backfield coach called Don and cautioned that he might be jeopardizing his football eligibility by boxing, even as an amateur. Don decided not to advance to other tournaments under the circumstances.

His grades were improving, although Psychology and Zoology were testing him. He still worked for two meals a day, which enabled him to get by on the GI Bill allowance. He began to think of buying a car if he could preserve his savings. Just when it seemed he was, indeed, getting on top of things, an unexpected intrusion occurred.

Before his second match in the Golden Gloves, Don had noticed a waitress from Morrie's sitting near ringside. She was a dark-haired, slim, and strikingly pretty coed. He had never talked with her at work because she seemed stuck up. Thus, it was a surprise to see her in this smoke-filled, noisy arena. Of course, once the bell rang, he had dismissed the matter. But there was more to come. As he departed Morrie's after work soon thereafter, she was at the exit. He held the door and followed her into the evening cold. When she seemed to be in no hurry, he continued beside her.

"I saw you at the boxing matches the other night," he said.

"I saw you, too," she replied. "In fact, I went to see you."

They walked on in silence. "Why'd you do that?" he asked. "I mean, come to see me box."

"I was curious."

"Curious?"

"Yes, curious."

They continued on, past the corner where Don should have turned toward his house.

"Where do you stay?" he asked.

"East Lawn."

"Mind if I walk with you?"

"That would be nice."

As they neared her dorm, she said, "I haven't enlightened you much, have I?"

"No, you haven't."

After a pause, she said, "At Morrie's you seemed more mature than the others."

"I had no idea you noticed me."

"Fooled you, didn't I?"

"That's for sure."

"When I read of your sensational victory in the paper, I decided to see for myself."

"What'd you think?"

"Brutal. Brutal in an intriguing way," she replied.

"You think I'm brutal?"

"No, I think you're insecure, though. You need to prove something."

"Isn't that why people do things?" he asked. "To prove something."

They had reached the dorm by then. He expected a polite "good night," maybe "thanks" for walking her home. Instead, she invited him inside. He followed her through the doorway, across a lobby, and down a stairway. She led him through the dim light to an overstuffed chair.

"Sit here," she whispered.

He settled into the chair and she sat more or less on the chair arm. An occasional giggle and murmuring indicated other couples were in the room under similar circumstances. Quite naturally she put her arm about his neck, an intimacy that pleased him considerably. What was this beautiful, perplexing creature up to? He tilted his head until their lips met. She responded warmly, knowledgeably, he thought. Somehow her body became draped across his lap as she toyed with the hair at the back of his neck. During the lingering kiss, his hand drifted to the warm curve of her hip beneath the coat. It had been months since he had last kissed a woman so passionately.

A few minutes later, the light came on. The intruder never came into sight; she simply had "announced" it was time to leave. They joined other departing couples wending their way outside. As Don paused near the entrance, she said nothing. No farewell, no encouragement, no words. "What a way to end the evening!" he thought. And then something occurred to him.

"Your name?" he asked. "I don't know your name."

"Libby," she said softly. "Libby Bowman."

She soon became a habit with him – and then an obsession! They would meet each night at closing and walk to her dorm. Frequently, they stopped for hot chocolate at a spot along the way.

Libby cleared up the mysteries by increments. She was twenty-one, had a degree in Sociology from Northwestern University and was now on a master's degree program in Psychology. Oh yes, she was an honor student, always had been.

Despite her trimness, she was not much for physical fitness. "As long as I look and feel good, why torture myself?" was the way she put it. She did enjoy walking and was intrigued by "adventures." One day she would like to go on an African Safari to observe the wildest of the wild in its pristine state.

Libby questioned the value of wars. She quoted Congresswoman Jeanette Rankin, lone dissenter in the Declaration of War in December, 1941, who had said "you can no more win a war than win an earthquake," to sum up her own views. Libby, herself, could never inflict harm on anyone or anything. But she did admire courage, although she did not consider herself courageous.

Her mother lived alone north of Chicago, having been deserted long ago by a wandering Roman Catholic husband. Libby had two sisters, one older and one younger. She was no longer close to her family because of a *misunderstanding*, which was not revealed.

In talking about himself, Don glossed over things that might make her think less of him. He said he had attended parochial school but did not dwell on the fact his family was Roman Catholic, lest her mother's prejudice jeopardize their own relationship. He glossed over depression-era experiences that had scarred his early outlook. He led her to believe that going to college was what he would have done all along; the war merely interrupted his plans. He did not tell her that he had volunteered for the Army. Yet he couldn't agree with her pacifism.

"Let me tell you a little story, Libby," he said one day. "A true story."

"In early 1943, we were in Tunisia. We arrived at a farmyard late at night, so we bedded down inside buildings. The next morning, we dug foxholes and cooked breakfast. One guy chopped down a tree and built a fire to heat water for tea. Chickens were running around, so one enterprising GI decided to change the menu. He killed and dressed a hen.

"In the midst of all this commotion, the French owner – we dubbed him Frenchie – drove up in a truck. Our presence shocked him, as did destruction to his property. Rather than confront Lieutenant, however, he chewed out his Arab workers for allowing this to happen. Somehow the blame settled on an Arab boy of about thirteen; perhaps, he was the selected culprit who had to be served up to mollify Frenchie. Anyway, the ruse seemed to work out well for everyone but the hapless lad.

"Frenchie pulled the boy's ears, pummeled him, and then booted him severely in the rear end. Other Arabs then joined in, pushing, shoving and heaping verbal abuse on the boy. When Lieutenant interceded, Frenchie stomped off in a huff.

"Later in the day, Frenchie came back and asked for Lieutenant. He now wanted to explain why he'd been so upset. It seemed that Frenchie had been a soldier in World War I and had fought in the trenches on the Western Front. He was bayoneted in the stomach and almost died. When he recovered after the war, he migrated to Tunisia with his wife. Eventually they had a son. Just when wheat farming was beginning to pay off, his wife died. When his son became a teenager, he yearned to go to Paris and meet relatives. Frenchie resisted at first but finally relented in 1939, just before war broke out again. Ironically the son was conscripted into the French Army and went off to fight Germans.

"Still, Frenchie felt he had made a prudent move. If he had remained in France the war would have taken everything. So in a way, he had escaped World War II – or so he thought! Then he arrived that morning and found soldiers killing his chickens, cutting down his trees, digging up his yard.

"What next?" he asked.

"The Germans," Lieutenant answered. "They're coming by here on their way to Medjez el Bab."

"You mean the Bosch have found me here?" Frenchie asked.

"Lieutenant nodded his head and Frenchie walked away.

"So you see, Libby, wars are like earthquakes: when they happen you have to deal with them." Don concluded.

"Maybe so," she said pensively.

Don doubted he had convinced her. Probably not. And he had to admit that he, too, sometimes questioned war-fighting, but he had found no alternative: In war you either win or succumb!

Don dodged discussing his academic record with Libby because she intimidated him on that score. But since she was a Psych Major, he brought up his shortcomings in Psych-I. "I understand readings and lectures but exams kill me," he told her. "Everything has a second or third meaning and I get tangled up."

She offered to help him, but preferred he ask questions. However, when he fumbled in formulating queries, he still came away feeling stupid. In the end he backed off and settled for more pleasing interactions in their relationship.

They would take long walks along the Iowa River and through contiguous parks. Don enjoyed being with Libby, talking with her, and marveling at her beauty. At times he would wonder what she saw in him, especially when they were apart. She seemed unaware of her hold on him, however.

They usually kissed goodnight among other couples gathered about East Lawn at curfew time. At times he touched her during long embraces, starting at her breast and working downward. She never interfered in his quest and seemed to enjoy such intimacies. He was careful not to go too far, lest she reject him.

Libby never mentioned former boyfriends until they made love the first time. On an unusually balmy day in early March, they ranged beyond usual routes. They crossed a field and came upon an empty hayrack along a fence in the midst of trees. He helped her up on the vehicle, then hopped alongside.

"This is a day for adventure," she said as they gazed upon the still-brown landscape.

"OK," he said. "But what?"

"Something we've never done before," she replied.

"Like what?"

"Have you ever made love on a farm wagon?"

"No."

"Neither have I," she said and turned to face him.

They kissed and lay back upon the open wagon bed. Her whole being became frenzied as she gave herself up. He, too, lost control and wildly groped her body. When she unabashedly welcomed his entry, he hesitated.

"I have no protection," he said.

"This is an adventure," she replied. "Who cares!"

He couldn't believe this was the controlled Libby who fascinated him so. She engaged him wholly with abandon. When he was spent, she clung to him with surprising strength. When her passion ebbed, they parted and adjusted clothing. They sat on the edge of the flooring and gazed outward once more. She was quiet, reflective. He was reluctant to say anything, lest he invite accusations of some sort. Women were known to do that afterwards. "That would be worse than rejection," he thought.

"Have you had many women?" she asked matter-of-factly.

"Some," he replied, not knowing how to treat such a personal question. And then, not really wanting to know, he asked, "And you, have you had other men?"

"You are the second," she answered readily.

He was taken aback – he had wanted her to say he was the first, despite her apparent experience. Still, he pushed on, asking whom the first had been.

"My mentor at Northwestern, a Sociology professor."

Noting his astonishment, she added, "You're not the first to be shocked. That *misunderstanding* alienated my family." Another piece of the puzzle had fallen into place; he waited for more, which soon followed.

"I would have married him but he had a wife and children," she added. "His wife would not free him, so I left."

"He took advantage of you," Don rationalized.

"Not really. There was no avoiding that first great adventure in my life."

"What was he like?"

"Very handsome. In his early forties, very bright, of course. Quite sophisticated and worldly. He had traveled a lot. Students loved him, especially the females during the war years. He was very persuasive, very articulate. I was not the first student he seduced, and I daresay not the last."

She was so straightforward, so unapologetic. Perhaps he could have dealt with it better if she seemed regretful, or somewhat disappointed.

"Nothing like me, was he?" Don asked.

"That's what attracts me to you," she concurred. "You are so opposite. You have courage, fierceness and physical strength. You live directly, experience life in real terms. His experiences are inferred, deduced and extrapolated from others. You are therapeutic for me. I need that to get beyond him."

Hearing that she needed him encouraged Don, but in a way she had used him, too.

"Now you know my secret," she said casually. "Tell me yours."

"Sure you want to know?"

"Certain."

"You don't know much about me, Libby," he confessed. "I've tried to impress you all along."

"I know that."

"You won't be too surprised, then," he began. "My first was in Scotland. She was a bit older and engaged to a British Naval Officer. Another guy and I were billeted in the house where she boarded in Dundee. I was in awe of her, but finally asked her out the last night there.

"She took me to her fiancé's house for tea. I felt awkward as hell, he being an officer and my being with his girlfriend."

"I'd say so," Libby commented.

"On our way home, we passed an overlook of a sort," Don continued. "The weather was drizzly and chilly. When I kissed her on the cheek, she turned about and opened her coat. I put my hands inside and nature took its course. Somehow we did it with her up against the railing. I said I'd marry her if she became pregnant, but she told me not to worry and wished me the best of luck. We sailed for Africa. I sent her a letter, but she never answered. She had simply sent me on my way with a jolly goodbye."

"A nice touch, that," Libby opined.

"I was good in Algeria and Tunisia, avoiding fleshpots and bars the few times I had off. I was still only nineteen and concerned about the future. We were in combat, so I prayed a lot, went to chaplain's services and all that."

Libby looked across the fields, tying to visualize what it must have been like for him.

"And then?" she asked.

"I saw my best friend killed in combat and wavered on the brink," Don continued. "But I still behaved up until we got near Cassino. Ever hear of the place?"

"Sounds familiar, probably from newscasts," she said.

"Well we were fighting near there in late 1943. We pulled back after Mount Pantano for a few days. A new lieutenant made me platoon sergeant because I had been around for a while. Anyway, another old timer and I sneaked off to a village called Alife. Chuck, the other guy, had met an Italian family there, name of Crotone. He had slept with one of the Crotone girls before. He knocked and they let us in. We had some wine and Chuck and the girl went off to another room– right in front of her parents! When we left, Chuck gave them all the cigarettes and lira we had and said we'd be back soon.

"We rejoined our unit and jumped off to cross the Rapido River a couple days later. The whole thing was a mess. We made it across in boats but couldn't get far beyond the riverbank. German artillery knocked out footbridges and trapped us. Enemy mortars and artillery pounded us all day. Chuck was killed right away. Then Lieutenant got it. I was tossed around several times but not hit badly."

He noted Libby scanning his face. It occurred to Don that she was analyzing him, comparing him to the professor who seduced female students and poisoned their minds with pacifism.

"You're so naive!" Don wanted to shout. "You think it takes courage to box? Not much, really! Anyone can get it up for a few minutes and fight like hell with padded gloves. Then the bell rings and it's all over. You go back to food, house, comfort and safety. Not so a rifleman," he continued the harangue within himself. "Even danger pales in the midst of drudgery that goes on for hour after grinding hour, day after grinding day, month after grinding month! When there's a lull, carrying parties tote off the dead and you don't even look to see who it is. Later you realize someone's not there anymore, so it was probably him."

Don heard his name called, fairly shouted out.

"Are you all right?" Libby asked when he snapped back.

He felt sheepish then. He had vowed not to have those lapses anymore.

"I haven't done that in a long while," he explained.

"Done what?"

"Drifted off."

He collected himself and went on: "After Lieutenant was killed, the Germans chased us back to the river. A few surrendered and the rest jumped into the Rapido where they drowned or caught on to something. I grabbed a floating log and drifted back across. I crawled out of the water after dark and headed away. I walked and ran to keep warm. I expected to run into our troops eventually but never did; I'd drifted too far down the river. I kept going, guiding on North Star.

"I came to a main road the next morning and hailed a deuce and a half. The driver was suspicious, so I told him what happened and that I needed to get away for a while. I told him he hadn't seen anything and he nodded. He dropped me off at Alife and I walked to Crotone's house. They didn't recognize me, I was so bedraggled and wild-eyed. But Marie, Chuck's girlfriend, gave me a blanket to wrap up in while my clothes dried. Papa Crotone gave me some warm wine and I fell asleep. Marie woke me later. I was in a bed in a dark room. She said I'd have to leave because Papa didn't want to be caught with a deserter in the house. He didn't want to turn me in, so it would be best if I just left.

"I told her then that Chuck had been killed and she broke up, wailing and crying something awful. She said Chuck had promised to marry her and take her to America after the war, which is why she went to bed with him. Now I had just said her ticket was no good.

"She forgot about my leaving. I guess she thought that maybe I'd substitute for Chuck, be another ticket to America. Anyway, she brought me some pasta soup, which I ate while she sat on the bed. I told her not to worry about MPs coming, because they thought I was dead, drowned, or missing in action. There wasn't a trace! Her English was good enough to get the message. She took my hand and kissed my forehead. I pulled the covers back and she crawled in. That was the first time I really made love. She was there for several hours and her family never bothered us."

"Was she pretty?"

"I don't know. The room was dark and I never really had a

good look at her before or after. She was dark haired and on the plump side, but who cared! She was warm and caring and I needed that.

"When I began to feel better, it occurred to me that my folks would be notified soon. Although I'd cut myself off, I didn't want Mom to go through that if it wasn't true. So, I pulled myself together, promised Marie I'd be back, and hitched a ride back to my unit. The new captain bought my excuse that I'd been lost because who could say I was wrong! Besides, the operation had gone so badly they just wanted to get beyond it. Like an earthquake, I'd say. Because there'd been so many casualties they hadn't reported me missing yet, either."

Libby was still analyzing Don, but he no longer cared. "Maybe now she'll be less idealistic about wars," he told himself. "Maybe now she'll realize her mentor doesn't know much about either wars or earthquakes. Maybe now she'll realize he's just an opportunistic lecher!" Don thought all those things, but he had no clue as to what Libby's thoughts were.

She was in a delightful mood as they walked back. When they parted, Don was more sure of her than he had ever been. Perhaps he had gotten through the cool facade she kept between herself and the world. Of course, this notion made the next day's events all the more confusing.

The first clue came when she did not show up for work at Morrie's. Then he could not find her at the usual meeting places. It was not like her to stay out of touch so completely. He walked to East Lawn that night and asked the receptionist to ring Libby. No response.

The next day was the same. On the third day he received a note through the mail. He ripped open the envelope and read:

> Dearest Don,
>
> I've gone to Evanston. Something unexpected! I will be in touch with you soon.
>
> Love, Libby

At first he rationalized. Perhaps her mother was ill or needed her. But as time passed he realized she had gone back to <u>him</u>! There had been more to that adventure than he realized or wanted to believe. After sifting through all the lovesick possibilities that might excuse her behavior, Don concluded Libby had ditched him.

In early March he decided to throw a party. He rounded up a

half dozen guys in the house and took them to the Airliner where he bought beer. It was a grand party as beer busts go. They got drunk and became boisterous. When the proprietor asked them to calm down, heated words were exchanged. The police came and the party-goers were taken off to jail.

The magistrate on duty was a boxing fan. He recognized Don from the Golden Gloves and released him and his friends on their own cognizance, but Don had to appear two days later. When he showed up, Don was fined $25 for disturbing the peace. Those at the house passed a hat and reimbursed him. Tatsuo Osaka tossed in a dollar, shook his head and smiled but didn't comment.

Then Bob Gotti called, said he had read Don's name in the Police File and wanted to know if Don wouldn't rather fight in the ring. It just so happened a State AAU Tournament was coming up in Des Moines. Don jumped at the chance and began working out the next day with Don Gotti and a couple other entrants. Being busy took Don's mind off Libby except in the evenings when they had usually met. "To hell with you!" he would mutter at such times.

On the first night of the tournament, Don fought the favorite, a boxer of high repute in the Midwest. Again, Don decided to take the fight to his opponent, not to let him up for air. It turned out to be a hell of a fight, the best of the tournament.

Don swarmed from the first bell and built up an early lead. Time after time Don's legs sagged as he took sharp blows to the head, but he never went down. Always he rallied and staggered his opponent in turn. At the final bell, both were hanging on. Don had won a split decision through aggressiveness. The next bout was anticlimactic and Don won the championship on a decision. The reward was a large trophy and a paid trip to the National AAU Tournament in Boston.

As things worked out, boxing took a back seat. Someone at Morrie's came up with Libby's address in Evanston; she had wanted her last check forwarded. Since Don was going by train, he would have to go through Chicago. Maybe he would stop and look her up.

The twenty-two hour train ride to Boston left the Iowa team drained. They roomed at the Manger Hotel, which was built around the Boston Garden where the tournament was held. Don lost his first fight and puked his guts out afterwards. "It's Rapido all over again!" he told himself. "A disaster!"

The most impressive fighter in the tournament was a sleek young

Negro light heavyweight out of East St. Louis, Illinois, named Bob Foxworth. Already he was being heralded as the "next Joe Louis." Don was tempted to stay and watch Foxworth fight again, but he decided to cut short his stay and return to Iowa City. He had another possibility in mind as well.

He had to change trains in Chicago, so Don took advantage of the hiatus and caught the L to Evanston. He booked a room in a nondescript hotel and then walked to the address where Libby stayed. A lady answered the doorbell and confirmed that Libby lived there, but she was out and wouldn't return until evening.

Don walked around Evanston until his feet blistered. He lunched and went to a movie. At seven p.m. he was back at Libby's house; however, she still hadn't returned. Don waited outside, walking back and forth so often he feared someone would turn him in for stalking.

Don was sitting on the steps of a nearby house when he spotted Libby entering her place. She was inside before he could intercept her, so he again rang the doorbell. The landlady answered, but Don looked past her and saw Libby standing in the foyer. She appeared somewhat perplexed and dispirited when she saw Don. The landlady invited him inside and departed.

Libby did not welcome him enthusiastically, but maybe she was just being proper in the presence of the landlady. However, when they went into a parlor-like room, they sat on a sofa as strangers would.

"Why did you come?" she asked with a hint of exasperation in her voice.

"I was passing through," he started to explain, then realized how phony that sounded. "I wanted to see you, to ask why you left," he continued.

"When I returned to East Lawn that day, there was a letter from him," she replied. "He said he needed me desperately."

"But you said you were over him."

"I thought I was, but when I read his note it all rushed back. I had to answer his call."

"What's the arrangement?"

"The same."

"You're his mistress?"

"I suppose the term fits."

"Did he leave his wife?"

"No."

"Libby, you deserve better."

She smiled, said nothing.

"Libby, I have a room not far from here. Let's go there."

"It's no use, Don."

He took her hands, drew her up from the sofa and put his arms around her. She responded listlessly. When he kissed her, she turned her lips away. He released her then and turned to leave. He wanted to say, "If you ever need me, I'll be there." Instead, he muttered "so long" and walked out. She followed, closed the door behind him and flicked off the outside light.

Don picked up his bag at the hotel and headed downtown to the railroad station. He was back in Iowa City at two a.m., determined to get on with his life – without Libby Bowman!

CHAPTER **IV**

A **CLEAR DIRECTION**

W hen Don Bauer departed Iowa City in June 1946, he wasn't sure he would return, ever. Successes and pleasantries had been offset by failures and disappointments. At times he believed the college campus was not for him. On the other hand, what would he do? There was no alternative, really.

Spring practice had dissolved one illusion in short order. Veterans who had spent war years playing football on service teams flocked back to campus. Dr. Eddie Anderson of Iron Man fame returned as head coach, and he knew talent when he saw it. Emlen Tunnel, Dick Hoerner, Earl Banks, et al quickly shoved aspirants such as Don Bauer off the field. Don didn't bother to turn in his gear; he let the equipment manager unceremoniously clean out the locker along with those of others disillusioned.

Semester grades were so-so. That his composition for the writing course was published in *Manuscript* – one of a dozen from two thousand papers considered – was a highlight. Don received an A in History, C in Zoology, D in Psychology, and C in Math. His overall grade point average was still below the minimum for participation in varsity sports. And he still had not decided on a major. Well, he could take care of that if he returned in the fall.

Then there was Libby! Just when he believed he had gotten beyond her, a letter arrived from Evanston. He was reluctant to open it; he didn't want to hear about him ever again. A whiff of perfume greeted Don as he removed the tinted pages from the envelope.

> Dearest Don,
>
> How fleet is a glance of the mind! / Compar'd with the speed of its flight / The tempest himself lags behind / And the swift winged arrows of light. / When I think of my own nature land,/In a moment I seem to be there; / But alas! recollection at hand / Soon hurried me back to despair.
>
> That's from William Cowper's Alone, and that's the way I think of you and the lovely hills and walks and sunrises and river

in Iowa City. To laugh and skip with you outdoors and our talks together are very sacred memories. I think I really love you - how could I have been so blind! I want to see you soon, very soon!

Love, Libby.

"Now what is she up to?" Don wondered. He went to the library and looked up William Cowper, an English poet who had lived from 1731 to 1800. The word "asylum" jumped off the page. Don read on. Cowper had been subject to bouts of acute depression. He attempted suicide more than once, and felt that he was damned by God for all eternity. "A very mixed-up person," Don concluded. "Perhaps that's Libby's fascination with him."

Don decided not to write until he heard more from her, but he did feel concern. Her involvement with the professor was not a soothing situation. By semester's end, Don had heard nothing further from Libby. "Could she have flipped out?" he asked himself.

When he told Tatsuo Osaka goodbye, Don concluded everyone was in a stew. Tatsuo smiled wanly and announced that he would not be back next year.

"My grades aren't good enough for dental college," he explained.

"What will you do?" Don asked.

"I will transfer to Michigan and take commerce," Tatsuo said. "My fiancée attends there now. Perhaps we will marry soon."

"I'm sorry dentistry didn't work out for you, Tatsuo. You had everything planned so well."

"It's worse than you think," Tatsuo continued. "Our parents are obstructing our marrying."

"Is it really their business?"

"In Japanese culture, yes. Definitely. My girlfriend's family is very wealthy and she has no brothers. Her parents want me to take her name so that their line goes on. That would insult my parents, however. Do you understand?"

"Sort of," Don replied, finding it difficult to believe such complications could arise in the United States. "I hope to see you again sometime, but if not, I wish you the very best, my friend."

They shook hands, Don picked up his suitcases and headed downtown where he caught a ride to Des Moines with the Gottis. Bob Gotti had arranged for Don to fight in a preliminary match in the Coliseum, along with his son. Don would get $30 for training expenses. Don knocked out his opponent, a flabby light heavyweight, in the second round. He picked up his money and went to catch a bus for Homesite. As he came out of the dressing room, he ran into – of all people! – Dad.

"What are you doing here?" Don asked.

"I came to see you box," Dad replied. "You did great!"

Don was tempted to ask "why now?" Instead, he said, "Come on, let's catch the bus and we'll talk then."

There were few other passengers, so they could converse openly. Don announced he was surprised to see Dad at the matches. "After all, you never came to my high school basketball games," Don reminded him. "I never understood that at all."

"We all make mistakes, Don. I shoulda gone, you're right. You know I did go to Brad's games. Never missed a one! That probably doesn't help you, though."

"It helped Brad. But worse than not coming to games, you put obstacles in my way."

"Like what?"

"I never had a decent pair of gym shoes, had to steal a jock strap and beg for a ride to games out of town."

"Well, we couldn't afford much in them days."

"I knew that, but you could have at least encouraged me."

"Don, you'd do things to upset me, too, which I never understood. Deborah and Frank never did anything like that."

"Sometimes I did, but I couldn't see why you let others push you around."

"I didn't know what else to do, Don. I gave up, I guess."

"Yeah and that infuriated me. You'd give up! Mom had to carry the load, put food on the table the best way she could. She got pretty desperate at times."

"We all got desperate, Don. That's the way it was."

"You didn't know how bad it was, really."

"What was so bad?"

"The hog."

"The hog?"

"Yeah, the hog."

"What about the hog?"

"I guess it was in 1936, when you went to see your brother. Frank and I rustled a hog."

"You did?"

"Yeah, we went hunting over along the north fence. We waited until dark and when a hog wandered by, Frank shot it. We dragged the damn thing through the fence and back home. Frank strung it up in the barn and we butchered it while Mom held the lantern."

"Well, I'll be damned. I had no idea…"

"You came back home and never asked where the fresh pork came from. I guess you thought God had pulled another 'loaves and fishes' miracle."

"Nobody ever said anything about that hog. But what could've I done if I'da known?"

"Probably nothing."

"Did anyone ever find out?"

"We didn't think so at first, but one day Frank and I ran into the neighbor in town and he kinda smiled and said, 'Been hunting lately, boys?' He knew, but he never did anything about it."

"Why didn't he go to the sheriff?"

"He felt sorry for us, I guess. But that wasn't the worst part. I had to face Father Conway. He was always so damned good to me! I swear, he knew I was hiding something. I would go to confession and couldn't bring myself to tell what I had done. What a mix-up that was! God, I felt guilty."

"Yeah, Conway was good. He'd always asked about you after you left. Made me feel funny, too."

"Tell me another thing," Don said after a pause. "Why'd you always send me to get the tobacco?"

"Tobacco?"

"The Prince Albert tobacco. When you had money you went to town. Other times, you sent me to 'charge it."

"Well, you never came back empty handed."

"Sometimes I was embarrassed, though."

"How so?"

"There'd be a couple guys hanging around Ernie's. When I'd ask Ernie to put it on the tab, they'd say, 'old man broke again?' Even Ernie might say, 'If I don't let him have it, he'll get his ass kicked when he gets home."

"Ernie'd say that?"

"Yeah, Ernie'd say that."

"But it would've been worse for Deborah or Frank. They

couldn't a handled it at all. They're more like me. You're like your mother. You'd always come up with something."

"Then it used to tick me off when you'd block anything I tried, like sell magazines or seeds or something."

"Well, people didn't like you pestering them. And everyone knew what our place was. No use trying to be more than that."

"Well, I learned in the Army that my place was what I wanted it to be."

"I guess you're right, Don. But you'll have to admit that I stuck around through thick and thin. I never took off like some guys did."

"But you threatened to. One night you had us all in a tizzy because you were such a failure and we'd be better off without you."

"I guess I was looking for reassurance. That's why I did that. I never woulda left, though. But you did! You cut out as soon as you could!"

"You think I wanted to leave?"

"You never showed otherwise. You never wrote anymore for a long time. What was we to think?"

"I was convinced at that stage I'd never make it back, so why drag it out?"

"So you gave up, too?"

"Yeah, I gave up. Lotsa times! But I always bounced back!"

"You're right there. When everyone was getting telegrams after Kasserine Pass I sorta thought we'd never get one. I figured you'd get away somehow, and you did."

"In a way, you did me a favor by treating me the way you did," Don said reflectively. "I was thrown back upon myself so much that I came to realize I didn't need anybody."

They rode in silence for a while.

"You sure about that, Don?"

"About what?"

"About not needing anybody?"

"Positive!"

They arrived in Homesite well after midnight. As they walked home, Don followed along in silence for a while. In a way, Don began to feel guilty about the way he had always regarded Dad. "Maybe he was doing the best he could," Don thought to himself. "Maybe now he's doing the best he can."

"Maybe I've been too hard on you, Dad," he said. "I've always had trouble accepting the way you do things, but that doesn't make you wrong necessarily."

"That's probably the best you can do, Don. I believe I understand you better now, at least better than I did before. I'm glad we had this little talk."

Don, too, was glad they had talked. By thus reconciling this part of his past, perhaps he could deal better with his future. Glancing northward, Don spotted Polaris shining bright and clear.

"Ready for a surprise?" Dad asked as he opened the kitchen door. He reached around the frame and snapped on a light – electricity! Inside, Don noted a brand-new refrigerator, a toaster and a radio! Dad was proud as he could be; Don had a lump in his throat. The shiny new appliances stood out starkly in the old farmhouse; they were indeed marks of progress!

The following day Don noted in a newspaper ad that American Smelting in Omaha was in need of unskilled workers. The company offered ninety cents an hour, a good wage for beginners. Don hitch-hiked to Omaha early the next morning and was dropped off after crossing Douglas Street bridge. Then he backtracked a couple blocks to the plant at river's edge.

He found the employment office and signed on. Within an hour he was assigned to care for six retorts. He followed instructions closely and soon managed to stoke the small furnaces with silver ore, coke and a dash of lime. Then he would plug the drain and turn up the heat. Every forty-five minutes he would break clay plugs and drain slag from melting ore.

The building was sweltering hot, with temperatures ranging from 110 to 115 degrees Fahrenheit, so Don was advised to "take it easy." He would service the retorts and then rest for fifteen minutes. By thus pacing himself, he took the heat in stride. The next morning, however, he found the GI coveralls he had worn crusted with salt from perspiration.

Don's supervisor, Ed Rolland, was easy to get along with. He was a mid-fortyish barrel of a man seemingly content with his job and lot in life. Periodically, Rolland tested the molten metal in the retorts. When it reached a prescribed purity, Don drained each retort into a heavy bucket and wheeled it to a huge basin. There, aided by a hoist, Don dumped the contents into a molten mass boiling at 2200 degrees F.

After three weeks of boiling and skimming, the silver ore was ready for pouring. Rolland asked Don to assist in this next step, whereby silver was drained into molds. After the metal cooled, Don jarred each ingot free of its mold and carried the 90-pound load to a weighing table. There Rolland and a representative of AJAX Silver Company weighed and stenciled each ingot.

Lugging several hundred ingots throughout the day was heavy labor indeed, but Don handled it readily enough. Rolland commended him frequently, and surprised Don with wage increase to a dollar an hour at the end of the first month. Overall, Don was satisfied with his summer work routine.

Social life was another matter, however. Don would shower on premises after work and turn in laundry at the cleaning plant. Then he would walk about Omaha until suppertime. He would eat at one of several family-style restaurants. Afterwards, he would go to a movie or walk some more. Then he would go to the YMCA and rent a bed for the night. If the Y was filled, he caught a streetcar to Deborah's apartment and slept on the sofa. On weekends, he would hitchhike to Homesite, see his family and go to a Saturday night dance. Sunday night he returned to Omaha.

Don tolerated this unwieldy lifestyle for seven weeks. On the first of August, however, he realized he was coming to decision time. The question still: "Would he return to college?" Summer was slipping by and he had found no alternative. Certainly, the smelting plant was not what he wanted.

Then unexpectedly one evening, Ed Rolland invited Don for supper. He accepted and rode home with Rolland after work. During the drive, Rolland again commended Don on his fine work at the plant. "You have a great future with American Smelting," he said.

Don felt uncomfortable in that he had misled his benefactor into believing Don was interested in a long-time job at the firm. His uneasy feeling increased when Rolland introduced Don to his wife as "my best worker."

Mary Rolland was a pleasant woman in her mid-forties. She fussed with food preparation and bustled to and fro, fixing everything just right while her husband and guest had a beer in the living room.

It struck Don that she was going to a lot of trouble.

A few minutes before they went to the table, a young lady joined them. Ed said, "This is our daughter...the best we have!" Her name was Betsy, and she was the Rolland's only child. Betsy was wholesomely attractive and appeared to be somewhat shy. She acknowledged Don with a slight smile and nod of her head. During the meal, she spoke only when addressed.

Afterwards, they went to a screened-in porch for dessert and coffee. As darkness gathered, Ed said, "Why don't you two go to a movie. Betsy, you take the car."

Thinking she might object, Don said, "Maybe Betsy has something to say about it."

She simply got up to leave. Despite the rather awkward beginning, Betsy relaxed as they drove away.

"Were you surprised?" she asked.

"By what?"

"Being coerced into a date."

"Your father was just being thoughtful."

"Oh, he's thoughtful all right. He wants me to marry some nice guy like you."

"I'm flattered."

Again she smiled, and then suggested they do something other than going to a movie.

"Like what?"

"Go to a bar, have a drink, dance."

"Sounds good!" he replied. "Do you know any places around here?"

"I know a couple."

Minutes later they pulled into a parking lot near The Elbow Inn. Don guessed she had been here before. Inside, several couples and a few singles sat at tables, smoking, drinking and talking. Sweeping jukebox lights sent shadows flowing across the ceiling. Betsy led the way to a table in a corner.

"I'll have a gin Collins," she told the waitress. Don ordered a beer.

"Would your father approve?" he asked when the waitress departed.

"Oh, he suspects I drink, but it's best he doesn't know for sure."

As the drinks arrived, someone put money in the jukebox and Frank Sinatra's "Night and Day" pealed forth. A couple went to the dance floor, fell into close embrace, and danced away.

"Do you dance?" Betsy asked.

"As you'll see, not very well," he said as he stood up.

On the floor, she settled nicely into his arms, her cheek against his.

"You're a good dancer," she said.

"Wait till they pick up the beat and you'll think otherwise."

"I like slow numbers best," she said. "It's closeness that's important."

As they returned to their table, she asked, "How am I doing so far?"

"You're attractive and saying all the right things," he said. "Besides, you're exciting."

She smiled again and sipped the gin Collins.

They had a second round and danced again. Don was thankful she apparently preferred slow, romantic numbers. He wanted the evening to go well. Not only was she the boss's daughter, but he was finding her company most enjoyable.

The old embarrassment came when she invited him to the floor for "Chattanooga Choo Choo." Don was heavy footed and couldn't pick up a routine she did very well. Don was now convinced Betsy knew her way around, more than her parents knew.

On the way home, she pulled along the curb on a quiet, dark street. She let the seat slide back and looked at Don. When he kissed her, she responded with parted lips. Betsy not only loved to dance, she loved to "neck" as well. In the dim light he observed the relaxed softness in her expression as he petted and fondled. Betsy was no neophyte here either – and she was in no hurry. However, she was the boss's daughter and it was getting late, so he suggested they call it a night.

"If you say so."

She turned on the roof light and fixed her makeup. "She is pretty," Don thought as he watched the graceful little motions of her hands. "Strong-willed, too!"

The Rollands were in bed when he and Betsy arrived back at the house.

"Thank your parents for a great meal and evening," he said as they stood in the driveway. "Maybe we can go out again."

"Give me a call," she said.

As Don walked to the streetcar stop, he checked his watch and noted it was eleven o'clock. Too late to go to the Y so he headed for Deborah's. He roused her out and slept on the sofa once again. Early the next morning he was back at American Smelting.

Ed Rolland was talking to another worker and seemed not to notice when Don punched the time clock. Taking over from the previous shift worker, Don went about tapping retorts as always. A half-hour later, Rolland walked up and said, "Good morning, Don. How are you?"

"Fine. And thanks for having me last evening. Your wife's an excellent cook."

"I'll pass that on to her," Rolland said. "How did you and Betsy get along?"

"Well, I had a good time, but she's a better dancer than I am."

"I thought you went to a movie!"

Don had given away Betsy's little deception! He did his best to recoup. "It was my idea," he explained. "I was afraid I'd fall asleep in a movie."

"I hope you didn't go to a drinking place," Rolland said. "She's under twenty-one, you know."

"It was all right," Don reassured his boss, but he had blundered. Perhaps seriously.

Rolland's behavior was pretty much what it had always been after the discussion. However, he dropped a couple things on Don. First, he asked Don to join the union, saying, "You won't go far in this business unless you do."

Next, he changed Don's work schedule. Instead of working daytime, he would now go to the four-to-midnight shift. Don begged off for a couple weeks, saying he would have to make new living arrangements. Rolland agreed but seemed reluctant to do so.

Now Don faced a dilemma. If he were to continue with American Smelting, he would have to join the union and pay dues. He also would have to buy steel-capped boots and a couple other items for safety. Adding pressure, he learned that Brad would be returning from the Navy in a week or so. Don dared not ask for time off to see his brother, yet he felt he had to. Then there were complications that grew out of a note from Betsy delivered by her father.

Don waited to read the message when he was alone. Betsy wanted to know if he would accompany her next Wednesday to a pre-nuptial party for a friend. Betsy would have the car and could pick him up where he stayed. If he accepted, Don was to say so on the back of the notepaper and give it to her father to relay back. After wrestling with a decision most of the day, Don scribbled that he would be pleased to go and that he would call her for details. Ed Rolland tucked the note in his pocket and wryly noted that he was now "messenger boy."

Over the weekend, Don picked up his dress clothes and returned to Deborah's apartment. She agreed that Betsy could pick him up there Wednesday evening. In fact, Deborah said Don could bring Betsy inside if they had time. Don called Betsy from Deborah's and completed the arrangements. Mrs. Rolland answered the phone and chatted merrily before relinquishing the phone to her daughter.

"Big date tonight," Roland commented when he saw Don.

"I don't know about wedding parties," Don replied.

"Oh, it'll be a nice gathering. In fact, it's a big party with music and everything. Those people are loaded!"

Betsy picked him up at six o'clock. They didn't have time to go upstairs, so Deborah never met Don's date.

Don was not comfortable at the event. Attendants were from affluent families, glib, confident and well dressed. His attempts at conversation were mostly futile; he was an outsider. He wondered about Betsy's place in this mix. She was a good friend of the bride but seemed to overreach when others came into play. There were drinks aplenty and Betsy freely partook. Don merely tasted the stuff, deciding to stay sober in case he had to drive afterwards.

When a dance number was to her liking, Betsy would tug him to the floor regardless of the beat. Don struggled to keep up, which didn't seem to bother her. In fact, she said he was improving. During slow numbers, she danced ever so close, overly affected, he thought. Since neither was really at ease, they broke away early.

Don offered to drive, but Betsy declined. She was in no mood to go directly home, so they drove to a secluded spot. They kissed and held each other for while, then she drew back and studied the lines of his face in the soft lighting.

"Do you like being with me?" she asked.

"Yes. Very much."

"Do you like me?"

"Yes."

She really kissed him then, and within the confines of the car they began petting. His hands roamed the warmth and softness of her body. She caressed and probed his work-hardened chest. Soon they were unabashedly seeking each other out. At fever pitch they pressed onward. She began to say mindless things. "Do you love me?" she asked.

"Yes," he replied.

"It's yours, Don. Everything I have is yours."

"I know, I know."

"But you must marry me. I cannot have you until we're married."

"I understand."

Although they continued to hold each other, lovemaking ebbed. "Why can't we?" she asked.

"Why can't we what?"

"Why can't we get married?"

"Because I have nothing to offer you," he said.

"I have no money, no job, no occupation, that's why."

"But you do have a job! Dad says you're doing very well. And as long as he's there you'll always have a job."

"There's more to it than that, Betsy."

"Such as?"

"Such as finding myself. What is it I am to do? What sort of profession or line or work for the long haul? Betsy, I'm not going to depend on others."

"But you can!" she interrupted.

"No. I have to put it together myself, and then I'll know where I'm coming from and where I'm heading."

"Sounds like a dodge to me."

"I don't think so. You don't know much about me. Your father doesn't either. He has seen just one side of me; I can be whatever I have to be for a while, but eventually I break out."

"What are your plans, then?"

"I guess I'm following Polaris."

"Polaris?"

"Yes, North Star. It keeps me on track."

Betsy was puzzled. "What does that have to do with us?" she asked.

"Everything!" he replied. "Right now I don't know where I am exactly but somehow sense it's about right. You see, Polaris isn't precise but it's unfailing! Betsy, there's something out there for me."

"How long does this wild-goose chase last?"

"I'll know when I find it," he insisted. "And you'll be the first to know."

Betsy was not impressed, nor was she convinced.

The following day, Don leveled with Ed Rollands, saying this had been a summer job all along. Now he would be going back to college in September. Don knew the reply would be painful, for Ed Rollands had treated Don decently – even preferentially. And, of course, Don liked Betsy.

"I believe you're making a big mistake," Rollands began. "Like I've said before, you have a future with this firm. I've worked here longer than you've been alive and have been treated well. I own my own home, my car, and dress my wife and daughter well. I've worked my way up, took no short cuts. But I got there.

"Now you," he continued, "want to get some place in a hurry. That's just not in the cards. I know you pretty well. You came from good, hard-working stock. Your folks took no short cuts either, did they? Don, face it! You're no book student, not from what you've told me about your grades so far."

"You may be right," Don replied, "but I want more than this and I'll find it. I appreciate what you've done for me, though."

"What about Betsy? She likes you, you know."

"I like her too, and I hope to go on seeing her."

"I'd rather you didn't," Rollands said. "She'd better go with some-one more predictable, someone who'll provide for her."

"If that's the way you feel, O.K. But tell her why it has to be this way."

Don picked up his due pay and hiked backed to Homesite. At least he'd now have time with Brad. After that, he would return to Iowa City and get a degree in something. That's what he would do!

Brad arrived home a day later, a bigger man than Don had ex-pected. The time in the Navy had matured him, of course, and pro-vided an opportunity as well. While serving with the Seabees in the Southwest Pacific, he had played a lot of baseball. Brad was left-handed and naturally turned to pitching. The coach knew a little about the game, so he was able to provide Brad timely advice.

The following Sunday, Brad pitched for the Homesite indepen-dent baseball team. Although a bit rusty, he nonetheless outclassed the opposition impressively. It so happened that a scout had dropped by and talked to Brad after the game. Brad was invited to Omaha to try out with a St. Louis Cardinal farm team.

This impressed Homesiters no end, and, recalling Brad's high school exploits, many predicted he was on his way. Brad, of course, was thrilled at the chance, but he was realistic concerning his chances in the very competitive, capricious game of professional baseball.

"I'm twenty years old now," he said, "and I have a lot to learn, things that kids in junior high are learning right now."

He kept his appointment in Omaha, and Don and Dad went with him. The scout and the Cardinal general manager put Brad through a series of throwing tests. He had a good, live fastball, a fair curve and acceptable control. Yes, he had possibilities, especially since left-handed pitching was at a premium. It was late in the season, but there was still time for him to join a Class D club somewhere. Within days, Brad was on his way to Frankfort, Illinois, for his fling at professional baseball.

Before he left, however, Brad rounded up a couple former high school classmates, one of whom had a car. Don joined them for a trip to some Omaha nightlife. But since all had been away, no one could think of a good place to go.

"How about it, Don?" Brad asked. "You've worked in Omaha all summer and must have touched some bases."

"There's the Elbow Inn," Don replied.

"The Elbow Inn, it is," Gordon Bleauvelt the driver announced, and he followed Don's directions to the parking lot.

As before, several couples and single girls were sitting inside. Don looked about to see if Betsy might be there, but she wasn't. When the jukebox played, Brad and Gordon asked two girls at a table to dance. When the girls accepted, Elmer Kellons, the fourth guy, surmised "folks here seem sociable."

"I brought a girl when I was here before," Don said. "I never paid attention to anyone else."

"Possibilities, possibilities," Gordon announced upon returning to the table.

"Yeah, I think we connected," Brad agreed. "Don, you and Elmer better stake something out, too."

Elmer nudged Don and said, "How about them two?"

Don turned to see two girls just arriving. One was Betsy!

"I think you're right, Elmer."

Don intercepted Betsy and asked, "Would you and your friend join us?"

Betsy was not only surprised but quite brittle as well. She asked her friend, Judy, if that suited her. Judy said, "That'll be fine." Betsy sat in the chair next to Don and Judy sat beside Elmer.

When music started, Don asked Betsy to dance. On the floor, she quipped, "I thought you couldn't dance!"

He ignored the sarcasm and asked, "How've you been?"

"Funny you should ask! And what brings you to Omaha?"

"I came looking for you."

"And what made you think I'd be here?"

"Polaris! See Betsy, it works!"

"Dad said to forget you. You're a dreamer. That's why he fired you."

"That's not how it was."

"Oh! How was it?"

"He got upset when I told him I was going back to college, so he cut me off."

"So, now Polaris is back over Iowa City where the cute little coeds are."

"I'm sure it sounds strange to you, Betsy. Sometimes it sounds strange to me, too. But let's drop that now. You see, this party was my brother's idea, but coming here was mine. And I was hoping you'd show up."

"Dad said you were through with me."

"That's his idea! I told him I wouldn't see you because he didn't want me to. But he can't stop me from thinking about you."

"I think of you, too," she said, softening.

"And I want to go on seeing you, Betsy. Who knows what'll happen."

At closing, Brad, Gordon and their dates went in Bleauvelt's car while Elmer and Judy went with Don and Betsy in her car. Betsy drove to a park where the couples walked off separately into the warm, quiet darkness. However, Betsy soon suggested they return.

"I don't want you to forget me, Don," she said when they were back in the car.

"I won't," he said.

"I want something to come of this, something that lasts."

"So do I."

As they embraced she whispered, "Touch my charms."

Through a tangle of clothing they petted feverishly in the front seat. Throughout, they pledged to find a way to be together – always!

They parted as Elmer and Judy approached from wherever they had been and whatever they had been doing. Betsy then drove back to the parking lot, where Brad and Gordon were waiting. Elmer told Judy goodbye and promised to call her next weekend.

"Write to me," Betsy whispered as she squeezed Don's hand. "I need to hear from you."

"I know," he said.

Brad left for Frankfort two days later. He said he would try to visit

Don in Iowa City, which couldn't be too far away. Maybe Brad, too, would go to Iowa University – if baseball didn't turn out.

Don helped Dad around the farm, readying the cribs for corn harvest. Frank was still in Missouri with his bride, but was planning on coming to Homesite for the harvest itself. In the meantime, Mom was trying to find a home for Frank and his wife. The first week in September, Don caught the train to Iowa City.

Don brushed off advice from the pharmacist that he "was wasting his time in a soft major" and decided to take Physical Education. He would follow that track, raise his grade point, and continue on a degree-earning program. At least he would come away with something – a degree in Phys Ed was something he did not now have.

Then, too, he would continue boxing. He did not contact the Wisconsin coach because Don's low grade point and participating in Golden Gloves probably had rendered him ineligible for Big Ten competition. Besides, he could now box for money in eastern Iowa and western Illinois, rather than just for glory in college.

During the summer, Don Bauer had cut through much of the clutter from his past. In the process, he had garnered some answers to nagging questions. Perhaps now he would define a promising path to follow in the years ahead.

Chapter V

On Track

The influx of veterans was staggering. To get an appointment with Dr. Cotter now took weeks! Cotter and his staff occupied a whole suite of offices to accommodate the increased workload. World War II ex-servicemen had taken over and the university was adjusting throughout.

Don found this trend encouraging. He was comfortable with veterans and he drew on their comradery and resolve to nourish his own pursuit of higher education. Despite the crowds, Don registered in his new major with little trouble. His advisor helped determine what subjects to take for a degree in Phys Ed. Don would carry seventeen academic hours, to include two sports that were not challenging. He added Spanish, History of Western Civilization, Economic Botany, and the second half of Written and Oral Communications. Don was confident he could handle this schedule, hold down a part-time job, and continue boxing.

He lived in the Quadrangle, a huge dormitory that featured two-man rooms. His roommate was Ed Banyon, a pre-law student and a veteran, who was quiet and older looking than his years. The route to classes took students through a picturesque valley, across the scenic Iowa River and up open lawns to Old Capitol – an inspirational trek, indeed! Overall, Don considered himself fortunate in this arrangement.

He checked with student employment and landed a dishwashing job at a drugstore lunch counter that would pay fifty cents an hour. Working two hours a day would provide him money for meals, especially if he smuggled a sandwich and a shake while working – a realistic expectation for student workers.

Don then looked up Bob Gotti, who was even more enthusiastic about boxing than before. Gotti said his son had trained all summer and would be fighting on a card at the local softball diamond that very night. Don accepted an invitation to accompany the Gottis to the matches. Young Gotti knocked out his opponent in short order. He had improved over the summer and matured as well. At nineteen, he had a bright future in the sport. "We're going to make a lot of money some day," his father predicted. "I'm glad you're back to train with him. You push him!"

The Gottis had a cozy arrangement with the YMCA gym supervisor, so Don joined them there the next afternoon at four p.m. He did calisthenics to loosen up, jabbed the light bag a bit, and then punched the heavy bag for a couple rounds. Next he sparred with young Gotti, who had a decided edge at that point. But Don Bauer used his size, fended Gotti off, and ended up satisfied with the drill.

"Same time, same place tomorrow," Bob Gotti announced afterwards.

Each morning, Don crossed the street from the dorm and jogged a couple miles on the university track. Then he showered, shaved and had breakfast. With his classes scheduled early, Don went to wash dishes at one p.m. Afterwards, he headed for the Y a few blocks away. It was a routine that left little time for socializing.

Don wrote to Betsy after he settled in. She responded promptly, hinting she would like to come to Iowa City for a visit. He filed this away, and began thinking of arrangements. Perhaps one of those cyclical visitor weekends would be best. He wondered what her parents' reaction would be.

Don's first bout was a three-rounder in Peoria, Illinois, against a Negro middleweight with Golden Gloves experience. Bill Blake was a well-built fighter and Don knew the match would be tough. The advanced billing gave Don a good buildup, which served to intimidate his opponent. Don wore his AAU championship robe to drive home the point as well. He wanted any edge he could get.

Both fighters were cautious in the first round. Don used his left jab to pile up points, while Blake aggressively rushed in with blows to the body. The second round would be crucial in this fight.

"Go for a knockout," Gotti advised between rounds. "And watch your gut! He's wicked down there."

The second round started slowly, but when Don ripped a left hook to the head, Blake charged in. Don had his back to the rope but managed to tie Blake up. After the clinch, Blake charged in again. Don fought him off this time, but couldn't land a solid blow. And so the round continued, with neither having a clear edge.

"You won the first, but he'll get the second," Gotti surmised in the corner. "Use your right more and hit harder. You're pushing up pillows!"

The last round was furious. Don rocked Blake repeatedly with left hooks to the head but couldn't drop him. Near the end of the round, Blake connected with a thunderous blow to the body. Don felt himself sag, grabbed Blake and held on. On the break, Blake again charged, flailing away to the ribs with both hands. Don was still trying to tie him up when the final bell sounded.

"He beat you," Gotti told Don in the corner. "He hurt you bad with that punch to the belly."

Actually, Don was awarded the decision, but he knew he was lucky to have survived Blake's onslaught near the end. Had Blake started sooner – been less hesitant at the start – he probably would have won. Nonetheless, Don picked up $35 for what one sportswriter called "the best fight of the evening."

The following day in Oral Communications, Don sat next to a tall, dark-haired guy with a ready grin and mischievous twinkle in his eye. Don had noticed him before; however, they had never spoken to each other.

"I hear you box," he said.

"Can't you tell by the black eyes?" Don asked.

"My name is Rob Stone," he said with a laugh. "And I've read about you."

After class, they walked to Whetstone's, a college hangout just off campus. Over a coke, Rob said that he had been discharged from the Navy because of a bad heart due to rheumatic fever. He had attended Iowa University before the war on a swimmer's scholarship, but, of course, swimming was out of the question now. Rob was an art major and had taken up golf.

When Don said he knew very little about golf, Rob volunteered to teach him. "I'm afraid golf's too tame," Don replied. "I'm better at contact sports, where I take it to my opponent."

"You'll learn to like golf," Rob promised. "We'll try it some time."

Although Don agreed to the offer, he was only half-serious. Besides not being really interested, there wasn't time. Nonetheless, their friendship grew as time went on. Rob was a likeable guy with puckish humor. His topic for an oral briefing was a description of his fiancée's physical endowments. The talk, rendered in risqué tones, was a hit, especially with veterans. The instructor, a young female grad student, was clearly discomfited, however. She managed to stay in control during class but gave in on her comment sheet.

"I question the accuracy of your fiancée's measurements – as you give them!" she wrote. "I believe your fantasies have prevailed!"

Nonetheless, Rob earned a satisfactory, and more! Apparently, his fiancée, Jan Dallas, was happy about the stir and rewarded Rob "in ways the instructor could only dream about," as he put it.

When Don later met Jan at coffee with Rob, Don agreed that Rob had not exaggerated much. Jan had a great figure! She was a second-year student in performing arts and intended to be a professional dancer. She also taught ballroom dancing at the Margot Rusel Dance Studio located just off campus.

Don mentioned that he could use dance lessons. Maybe if he knew more about the art, he wouldn't feel so awkward on a dance floor.

"I know the feeling," she said. "Dancing is a great confidence builder. You should take lessons."

"I'm not sure," Don replied. "Not only am I slow, but I'm para-noid too."

"You'll get over that," she promised. "Rob was a klutz until I taught him. Right, honey?"

Rob pinched Jan's thigh beneath the table, smiled impishly and said, "She taught me a lot, Don. Believe me! But don't overlook golf – mastery of the game is a great confidence builder, too."

Since golf courses were closing in mid-October, Rob's session could be gracefully postponed. Since dancing was more popular in winter, Don could hardly avoid a session with Jan. However, boxing was taking more of his time than he wanted. Gotti came up with matches every couple weeks, and purses were increasing seductively. As Don continued to win, he was inclined to take the fights —and the money! Then, too, his reputation grew and Don liked the attention his prowess attracted. Even though boxing was outside the purview of the univer-sity, Don was nonetheless "somebody on campus."

In early November, Bob Gotti received an offer for Don to fight Bill Blake again in Rock Island, Illinois. The promoter would pay Don $50 for the semiwindup on a card featuring young Gotti. Don would be ready for Blake this time. Don worked on his midsection, increasing sit-ups and taking a pounding from the medicine ball heaved by Bob Gotti. During sparring sessions, Don Gotti worked to Bauer's body as well. Finally, Don built stamina by increasing roadwork.

As events unfolded, Don's training was misdirected. Bill Blake didn't show the night of the fight, so the card was rearranged. When

Don and a heavyweight, Clyde Claiborne, were left without opponents, Bob Gotti volunteered Don to fight Claiborne. Don questioned fighting someone who outweighed him by thirty pounds, but Gotti had an answer.

"Don," he said, "you match him well. Just as tall, just as long in reach and just as big in the shoulders. All that weight is in Claiborne's legs, and it slows him. You'll take him easy!"

Was Gotti serious?

Don wasn't reassured when he met Claiborne at ring center for instructions from Al Nemow, the referee. Clyde Claiborne was massive!

"When I say 'break,' I want you both to step back and break clean," Nemow admonished. "And, remember, protect yourselves at all times!" (This last instruction would be critical in this fight.)

Gotti advised Don to stay away and jab the heavyweight "crazy." However, Claiborne had other ideas: He tried to overwhelm Don, befuddle him, and wear him down. Don had trouble handling the bull-like rushes, so the first round – more wrestling than boxing – drew a smattering of boos from a disappointed crowd.

"You act scared!" Gotti chided in the corner. "You're fighting his fight! You gotta take charge, do you hear me?"

Don couldn't respond; he was still gasping for breath from this futile effort to match strength with the bigger man.

"Now listen up!" Gotti snapped. "He's leaving himself wide open, so after a clinch don't step back. Hook him hard!"

The bell rang and Gotti jerked the stool away. Claiborne rushed in once more and Don tied him up as booing started up again.

"Break! Break!" Nemow demanded as he pushed them apart.

Claiborne dutifully stepped back but Don held his ground. When Claiborne dropped his gloves – as Gotti said he would – Don shot forward and smacked him with a solid left hook. Claiborne toppled like a felled tree, sending up puffs of dust from the canvas.

Nemow seemed at a loss, but when the crowd roared approval he picked up the count as Claiborne's corner man shouted, "He hit on the break! He hit on the break!" A perplexed Clyde Claiborne was on his feet at the count of nine.

Don jabbed a couple times and followed with a straight right to the chin. Again, Claiborne went down and the crowd loved the spectacle. Gamely, Claiborne got up at nine and motioned for Don to come on. Don feinted a right-hand lead and drove home a vicious left hook. Clyde Claiborne didn't bother to get up this time, even though he was not hurt so much as embarrassed.

"Didn't I tell you!" a jubilant Bob Gotti shouted to Bauer, who was as shocked as anyone in the arena.

Don passed through cheering fans on his way to the dressing room. He couldn't help feeling exhilarated. Maybe Don Bauer was good! Maybe his left hook did have the kick of a mule! Maybe he, too, could make a lot of money fighting in the pros! After dressing, he returned to watch young Gotti win a decision in the main event.

Just outside Rock Island on the trip back to Iowa City, they stopped at a steakhouse for something to eat. Don was surprised to see Al Nemow standing at the bar. He and Bob Gotti obviously knew each other well, for they exchanged good-natured barbs while they drank. Both were in high spirits. At some point, Gotti agreed to give Nemow a ride to Iowa City, where he could catch the trolley on to Cedar Rapids.

Young Gotti drove with his father sitting alongside in front. Nemow and Bauer were in back. Bob Gotti had a bottle in his equipment bag and some mix from the steakhouse. With tongues loosened, both spoke freely.

"You hit him quick, Don," Nemow ventured. "I heard the crowd cheer when you decked him, so I said, Hey! I didn't see nothing!"

"He dropped his hands," Don explained.

"Hey! You made it a hell of a fight!" Nemow allowed. "And you got away with it! That's what counts: You got away with it!"

"You know something, Al," Bob Gotti interjected. "He did just what I told him to do. Right, Don?"

"Why you sly sonofabitch!" Nemow yelled. "I shoulda known."

Bob Gotti smiled smugly.

"Let me tell you something else, Bauer," Nemow said after a pause. "You gotta screw your friends, cause your enemies won't come close!"

"I like that," Gotti senior responded as he passed a freshened drink back to his pal. "You gotta screw your friends. Sounds good to me!"

As Don withdrew from the drunken conversation, he became aware of cigarette smoke wreathing about his head. "What are smokers thinking of?" he wondered. Even young Gotti smoked, yet he wanted to box big time! When he thought of the addictive side of smoking, Don was reminded of another group of smokers in another place at another time.

Early on November 8, 1942, Don Bauer's Commando unit headed toward shore east of Algiers. The moon dodged in and out of clouds as fragile landing craft battled choppy seas. Those on board fought off seasickness as they crouched on sloppy decks under heavy combat loads. Periodically, a French coastal gun fired away at Allied ships anchored offshore.

When landing craft grated on sandbars still hundreds of yards from the beach, nervous sailors dropped ramps and GIs scrambled off into the sea. Initially salt water was waist deep, but it deepened as they struggled shoreward. Taller men helped those shorter across deep spots, sometimes with water over their heads. Eventually, Americans reached shallow water and, ultimately, the beach

When they paused later, GIs realized they had no smokes. Even those cigarettes wrapped in cellophane and stowed inside helmets were soaked through with salt water.

"No way to salvage those babies," one GI lamented as he tossed sodden cigarettes away.

He was right, of course, and throughout a long day of fighting, marching, and counter-marching, American soldiers had no tobacco.

Don was thankful he had never engaged in this particular rite of passage. For one thing, he couldn't afford to smoke while in high school, and then he thought that not smoking might give him an edge in basketball. If this early resolution needed reinforcement, the anguish he witnessed on Algerian shores would do.

Don was awakened when they dropped him off outside the Quad at one a.m. He had to be at classes in a few hours, so he tried to re-orient his thinking toward academics. Then, too, he had to make up his mind on Betsy's visit or else forget about her. At the moment, last summer was a long time ago.

With approaching holidays, boxing demands tapered off. Don still joined the Gottis every other day at the Y for a relaxed workout, just to keep in shape. He continued running every morning as well. However, during this lull he decided to take up on Jan's offer.

He stopped at the Margot Rusel Dance Studio one afternoon. Group lessons were in progress on the main floor, while one-on-one instruction was taking place within cubicles to the side. He surveyed the scene from the entrance and spotted Jan. When she noticed him, she dismissed her student and approached Don.

"Well, look who's here!" she said cheerily.

"I'm just looking this over," he explained. "I still haven't decided, though."

"Let's decide right now!" she said emphatically. "You *will* take lessons from me and we start today!"

She then led him to a cubicle before he could protest too much. On the way, Don noticed other men looking Jan over, but she appeared not to notice. She obviously knew how to deal with overly attentive males. The cubicles had some privacy afforded by four-foot-high walls and glass above to the ceiling. Don felt uncomfortable with everything, including the gleaming hardwood floor.

"This must cost a fortune," he conjectured. Still, he preferred to be away from critical eyes while he took lessons.

"What's your interest?" Jan asked.

"Popular stuff. The Lindy, Foxtrot, and Rumba." Don replied.

"Let's start with the Lindy," she said, placing a record on the phonograph. "Chattanooga Choo Choo it is!"

Jan demonstrated steps and rhythm. "Slow, slow, quick-quick," she announced, stepping forward with her left foot, stepping in place with her right, and quick-stepping left and right in sequence. She made the repetitions look easy and inviting. He was encouraged when he imitated her movements reasonably well. And he had to admit she was inspiring.

Jan Dallas looked good and knew it! Her movements were effortless; each step, tap and turn was sheer grace. Jan "lived" the music and "acted out" the rhythm. Her tawny hair tossed saucily with the Lindy beat. Her blue eyes sparkled and her lips flashed a bewitching smile as she danced. With his left hand at her waist, Don felt thrilling firmness beneath the flimsy cloth. He sensed she was aware of his excitement.

"Was that so terrifying?" she teased when the music stopped.

"So far, so good."

"Now the Rumba."

Jan's mood turned sultry at the start of Cole Porter's <u>Begin the Beguine</u>. She adjusted to closed position and placed his right hand at her waist. She swayed sensuously, coaxing the rhythm: "Quick, quick, slow; quick, quick, slow." Again he picked up the basic routine readily.

"You're a fast learner," she opined when the record had run its course.

"No, you're a fast teacher," he replied.

She seemed pleased with the results. He was pleased at how well things had gone overall. They agreed he should continue. She said things could be arranged so that lessons wouldn't cost him "an arm and a leg."

"But there's fine print," she added mischievously.

"Oh, oh," he feigned shock. "The other shoe drops."

"Modest enough though. I want to see you box some time."

"I'm flattered you are interested."

"And why wouldn't I be?"

And so rapture took flight. So easily, so naturally, so flippantly.

When Don mentioned the fine print in class the next day, Rob was not enthused. He dismissed Jan's remark as "one of those crazy things she comes up with." Don suspected then there was something he didn't know about Jan and Rob's relationship. Still, he continued dance lessons with Jan but did not discuss them with Rob.

For the third session, Don dressed up, wearing his best slacks and a shirt that seemed appropriate for dancing. He also wore shoes with leather soles, polished, too. He felt at home now as they added Foxtrot and practiced Lindy and Rumba.

Although Jan had a flirtatious quality, she was a stern teacher. She rebuked Don if he turned frivolous – dancing was serious business! She rewarded him by increasing the complexity of routines, never letting him believe that he had mastered much. She worked on posture and style. She took him to a movie to watch Fred Astaire and Ginger Rogers. Although he held her hand during the movie, the gesture seemed innocent enough. And never did she mention paying for lessons, even when he asked for a bill.

"I want you to be indebted," she would laughingly reply when he offered to pay up.

Don was so involved with academics and activities that he never followed up with Betsy. In fact, he didn't go to Homesite for Thanksgiving; rather, he spent the day with Rob's family who lived in a small town near Iowa City. Of course, Jan was there, too. It wasn't until Christmas that Don got around to Betsy, but by then his interest had been diverted.

Just before leaving campus, Don went to a Christmas party at Margot Rusel's. Besides decorations, Margot provided refreshments, including spiked punch.

Don was Jan's student guest for the evening. She wore a bright red dress that flared at the waist. For the first time, Jan set aside her insistence on perfection and let Don lead naturally. He marveled at how readily she anticipated his every move. "I couldn't step on your toe if I tried to," he said; she smiled.

When <u>Begin</u> <u>the</u> <u>Beguine</u> played, they excelled. Her eyes never left his as Don and Jan rendered their version of the sensuous number. When they moved to closed position and slithered in place, others stopped to watch. And when she spun away, only to wrap back into his arms, others applauded. "You've really caught on," she said afterwards.

"It's you, Jan. You'd make anyone look good."

Yet he did feel good about himself. Jan liked him – a lot! And he liked her, too. At the moment, neither thought of Rob Stone. When Don left to catch a bus for Homesite after the Christmas party, she walked him to the foyer. Out of sight, they held a goodbye kiss for a long while.

"Hurry back," she whispered. "We have more to do."

He patted her and departed. Don Bauer needed time to sort this out.

He approached Christmas holiday in Homesite with ambivalence. On one hand, he wanted to see his family and take a break from a hectic schedule. On the other, he didn't want to leave what he had put together in Iowa City. Don Bauer was on track – for the time being at least.

CHAPTER VI

CLEARING THE COURSE

A telephone had been installed at the Bauer's in Don's absence; the postwar waiting list was working itself out. Even though the Bauers were on a party line, Mom was highly appreciative. With the phone she had achieved just about all the material goals she had ever envisioned for herself. The Bauers owned their farm, had a comfortable house and were blessed with conveniences.

"God has been good to us," Mom concluded.

"You deserve it, Mom," Don added.

When Don called Betsy the following morning, Mary Rollands answered. She said Betsy was not there, so Don left his phone number. However, he wasn't sure Betsy would return the call, judging from the tone of her mother's voice. Mary Rollands seemed just a bit uptight. Oh well, it would simplify matters if Betsy didn't call.

The next morning Betsy called all right. Her manner was guarded, but when Don asked when they could get together, she said, "Whenever you can make it."

"I'll be down tomorrow, about noon."

"That will be fine."

"I need a car," he told himself. "Next summer I'll have a car."

He caught a bus to Omaha the next day and arrived at the Rollands' just before noon. Betsy greeted him at the door and asked him in. Mrs. Rollands was friendly and chatted briefly. Then he and Betsy in her car went for lunch. As before, once they were alone she talked freely. "I didn't expect to hear from you again," she said.

"I've been busy, especially with boxing."

"I don't know why you box," she scolded. "The risk is too great for whatever you get out of it."

He dodged by asking, "So what have you been up to?"

"I'm seeing someone else," she announced.

"Is it serious?"

"Could be. We get along well and Dad likes Dick. He was in the Army, too."

Don wanted to tell her about Jan, but then Betsy might think he was trying to upstage her. Besides, if Betsy wanted a graceful way out, Don would let her have this one.

They had a sandwich at a burger place, which was not crowded and they could talk. Betsy said her father was doing great, but he never mentioned Don Bauer any more. Of course, no one in the Rollands family mentioned Don Bauer anymore. After lunch they drove to a park now desolate and deserted in winter. They walked about in the breezy, cool weather. Dick, her boyfriend's name, came up often in conversation. He was an auto mechanic, and a "good one." He was older than Betsy and had been married once before; however, his wife had run out on him when he was away in service.

"That happened," Don offered.

"I know it did," Betsy said. "And I suppose it couldn't be helped, especially during long separations. Wars are destructive in more ways than one."

"Yes, they are."

When they returned to the car, she was in no hurry to leave. When they kissed, she seemed as fervent as before. However, when he attempted to go further, she restrained him, saying, "Not now."

He figured she was confused, so he didn't persist. They talked naturally on the way to the bus station, where she dropped him off. He said he would call her again, and she said that would be fine. A couple days later, he received a note:

Dear Don,

This is to tell you not to call me again. I hope you won't be angry with me, but I know now that it's Dick. I had to see you once more to be sure. Now I am sure. I wish you well in the future, whatever you do. I hope you stop boxing, for your own sake. Already I can see that it has changed your face and perhaps you have been injured in other ways. I do not want anything bad happening to you.

Fondly, Betsy

He folded the letter and put it away. He would read it several times over the next few days. Betsy was appealing, and he regretted that more had not come of their relationship. On the positive side, a complication had been removed from his life.

Brad came home for Christmas. After the baseball season, he had stayed in Frankfort, Illinois, where he took a job working for City Utilities. It was not much of a job, but it would tide him over until spring training, which is what the city had in mind. The baseball-minded community wanted him back.

It was a lively holiday at the Bauers. Deborah announced her wedding plans for next summer. Frank and his wife announced they were expecting a baby in the spring. Jeanne announced she was class president and doing well with her schoolwork. Brad announced he would do well in pro ball, and Don announced he was holding his own. Dad was beside himself with pride in his family, and Mom led them all in giving thanks to the Lord.

They attended a New Year's Eve dance in Homesite. Don surprised everyone with his improved dancing and shocked Jeanne when he could keep up with her jitterbugging. In fact, Jeanne tugged him onto the floor more than once, turning down bids from classmates.

"I can dance with them anytime," she said. "I can only dance with my brother when he's here – and that's not often!"

Don returned to Iowa City on January 3rd. Brad rode the bus with him and stayed overnight in the dorm before going on to Illinois. They had a chance to talk about the future, and Brad repeated that if he didn't make it in baseball he would surely come to Iowa City too.

"I'd like to take what you're taking, Don," he said. "I've always wanted to be a high school coach."

"If it comes to that, I'll still be here," Don promised.

Don was disappointed to find the dance studio still closed for the holidays. In fact, it wouldn't open until January 6th, which meant he wouldn't see Jan until then. Rob wasn't in class for the first Oral Communications session, so Don missed hearing about Jan indirectly as well. Then he had a bit of luck. Or was it fate?

He went to the coffee shop that he and Rob frequented, and Jan was there! She was with Billy Mickles, a male dance instructor, but beckoned Don to join them. After meeting Don, Mickles excused himself and departed.

"Where's Rob?" Don asked when they were alone.

"He's had the flu, which can be serious with his condition."

"Sorry to hear that."

"Well, my holidays weren't exciting," Jan continued. "How about yours?"

"I had a good time, but I missed Iowa City."

"Do you have a girlfriend back home?"

"Not anymore. She gave me a 'Dear Don' for Christmas. She'd met another guy since last summer and he won out."

"Are you broken up over it?"

"No. I'm sort of relieved."

Jan smiled and patted his hand. "What are you doing this evening?" she asked. "There's a movie I'd like to see."

"Let's go!"

They agreed to meet at the theater. The Best Years of Our Lives was playing, and although Don avoided wartime movies he looked forward to seeing this one because it dealt with readjustments of World War II veterans. In the meantime, Don called Bob Gotti and learned that he could be on a fight card in Cedar Rapids in about three weeks. Don agreed to the match against an unnamed opponent.

Jan and Don sat in the center near the back of the theater. She liked movies, especially war stories. She sat close and they held hands throughout – except when she dabbed her eyes during crying scenes. Once he put his left arm around the back of her seat and she leaned closer. Afterwards, they stopped for hot chocolate and then walked to Aunt Becky's house where Jan stayed. When he told Jan about the upcoming fight, she said she wanted to go.

"O.K., I'll get tickets for you and Rob," he promised.

"One thing, Don. Let him think it's your idea."

"I understand."

He kissed her goodnight and trotted all the way to the Quad. Don Bauer had training to do: This was one fight he wanted to win convincingly! Of course, dance lessons were now put on hold.

Don had reason to be apprehensive. The Cedar Rapids Gazette sports page carried a large picture of his opponent, Nick Bozano, who said he was looking forward to beating Bauer. The promoter also said Bozano would win, probably by a knockout. Don knew this was hype, but he knew nothing of Bozano's record. All Don could do was prepare for the worst, so a bit of worrying was in order. Over the next two weeks, he put everything he had into training and mental preparation.

Rob Stone accepted the tickets readily, but said he would have to ask Jan if she could get away that night. "She's awfully busy, you know."

Before leaving for Cedar Rapids, Don went by the studio to see Jan.

"Of course, we're going!" she said. Then noting his nervousness, she kissed him and said, "You'll win, I'm sure."

"She has no idea what I go through before a fight," Don muttered aloud as he walked to meet the Gottis. "No one does!"

Don was razor sharp. He kept Bozano off balance with left jabs and parried most of the Italian's wild punches to the body. Near the end of the first round, Don connected with a surprising left hook to the jaw. Bozano went to the canvas with a thud. He was still groggy when the bell rang.

"You've got him where you want him," Bob Gotti shouted in the corner. "Now take him out!"

Don started the second round jabbing, jabbing, and jabbing. Then he nailed Bozano with a straight right, then a left hook, then another right and down he went. The referee stopped it without a count this time. Thus ended the fight of Don Bauer's life.

He hurriedly dressed and went looking for Jan and Rob. He found them in the balcony when Jan waved to him. She clutched his hand to let him know she was proud. Rob, too, had been impressed. "You're a tiger!" he said.

Don put his arms around both and said, "Thanks for being here."

Jan leaned her hip against Don and kept it there. Reflexively, he dropped his hand and drew her closer. Rob, intent on the fight in progress, was unaware of this exchange.

After Oral Communications the following morning, Don and Rob met Jan for coffee and doughnuts. Jan's inordinate attention discomfited Don, but Rob seemed not to mind. As they broke for the next class, Jan asked when he would resume dance lessons.

"Give me a couple days," Don replied dismissively.

By mid-afternoon, the fight had caught up with Don. He went to the dorm and crawled into bed. At some point he heard his roommate come in, but that was it. He slept through until the next morning. Sore and stiff, he dragged himself to the shower and stood under the hot water for a half-hour. His whole upper body hurt from bruises inflicted by Bozano's wild swings. And this had been an easy fight!

That afternoon, Don loped around the track to loosen up, and then he did calisthenics in the field house. That evening, he went to the dance studio in a well-timed move.

"Let's go somewhere else," Jan said when he arrived.

It was dark when they reached Aunt Becky's house. Jan opened the door and he followed inside. She turned on a hall light and removed her coat. She took his hand and led him down the hallway to her room. Inside, she turned the lock and faced him.

Don held out his arms and she melded against him. She kissed his face and ran her fingers through his hair. He roamed her body, hand first across her breast and then down her back to curves below. He rubbed gently but insistently. She reached inside his loosened shirt to caress his battered body. Dull pain and soreness gave way to titillation. Aroused, he placed her upon the bed where she accepted him eagerly. After a few seconds of frenzied passion they lay quiet – his weight full upon her.

Then he lay back and she snuggled against him. As he stroked the small of her back, she said, "I've loved you for a while."

"I know," he whispered. "But I've always loved you."

"Always loved me?"

"Yes. You're what I've wanted all my life. Polaris led me to you."

She smiled, thinking he had indeed been carried away.

Eventually, reality intruded. "What about Rob?" he asked.

"We broke off our engagement."

"When?"

"This morning."

"Why?"

"You have to ask?"

"Because of me?"

"Yes."

"You told Rob that?"

"No."

"But he knows?"

"Yes."

"What do we do now?"

"We let nature take its course."

At the next class, Rob sat away from Don. He chatted with those around him and seemed unperturbed. Don decided to avoid confrontation. He would go about things normally, and, indeed, "let nature take its course."

End-of-semester exams and registration took up Don's time and resolved the dilemma of facing Rob Stone in class. Don earned a B+ average and Satisfactory in Oral Communications. After that, he saw Rob only in chance meetings about campus. In those instances, they spoke and passed.

Don and Jan met regularly, working around schedule conflicts. He went to the studio twice a week for lessons, as they worked on the Waltz, Mambo, Cha-Cha, Samba and swing. Often they went to movies on weekends. Occasionally, they walked about the city, visited the art centers or independent exhibits. At times they studied together in the library. Don liked being with Jan and being seen with her; she attracted attention wherever she went.

Aunt Becky, a piano teacher in the University music department, often worked evenings, so they frequently slipped into Jan's room to make love. When he asked about contraception, Jan told him not to be concerned. She was free and imaginative about sex, and he relished her openness. They lost themselves totally when they loved, evoking fantasies throughout. Although they regularly proclaimed love for each other, marriage was never mentioned. Of course, they never lost sight of what had brought them together dancing. As he improved, they turned to dancing for fun and show.

Periodically, big bands were booked at the Student Union. Jan and Don passed up the Beaux Arts Ball – too far out – but, they decided to attend the University Prom in mid-March. Raymond Scott's Orchestra was scheduled and Jan thought his music would suit their style. When they practiced at the studio, Jan groomed Don for his role as leader.

At the same time, Don had accepted an offer to box on a sponsored team in the Cedar Rapids Golden Gloves Tournament in early March. He would receive $50 under the table for training expenses.

Don was confident he would win the middleweight division, but he took no chances: he trained relentlessly. Since little was known about opponents in Golden Gloves competition, a boxer had to be ready for just about anything. Don's preparation paid off.

He outpointed an awkward neophyte in his first fight. Then, he was awarded a technical knockout in the semifinals and won a clear decision in the finals for the championship. Thus, he was eligible to go to Chicago the following week for the Midwest Championship fights. Chicago, of course, was a well-known boxing center, so competition would be a notch keener. However, Don had beaten several of the Midwest middleweights already and felt his chances were good.

Don Gotti won the welterweight division, so Bauer would travel with the Gottis to Chicago. They would leave on the coming Tuesday, but before that Bauer had a date for the University Prom.

He wore a dress suit that matched Jan's black sequined sheath formal that fit like a glove. He gave her a red carnation, which she put in her hair. As they entered the Union, Don noted admiring glances from both men and women - Jan was a "stunner." He couldn't help feeling a bit overmatched in this setting, but she reassured him.

"We'll do well," she promised.

"Easy for you to say," he rejoined. "You have red carnations, I

have black eyes!"

She laughed and said, "Look at it this way: I'm with the best boxer at the ball!"

Despite her outward poise, Don detected slight nervousness. He rationalized this was natural, similar to his own tension before a boxing match. Dancing was her "competition," and she was a perfectionist. Then, too, she knew others would be watching critically, but he never doubted she would acquit herself well.

The orchestra started with "Yellow Bird," a Cha-Cha. Couples hesitated to move onto the floor, but not Jan and Don. He was comfortable doing the Cha-Cha, and he loved showing Jan off. She was up to the challenge and her interpretation of the number drew attention. Although the floor became crowded, Don and Jan always had space and an audience! Rumbas, Waltzes, Lindys, Foxtrots, Cha-Chas, they rendered an original version of each.

Afterwards, they stopped for a hamburger and shake and then went to Jan's place. She held a finger to her lips as they tiptoed down the hallway to her room. They lay on the bed together with clothing removed, reliving the enchanted evening. She nestled with arm and leg draped across his body as they talked in lowered voices.

"What are you thinking?" she asked.

"How blissful this is. I can't believe you happened to me."

"Why can't you believe?"

"It's all so improbable."

"Why do you say that?"

"I can't believe you love me. It's *Pygmalion* in reverse!"

She thought about that for a while and then said, "You are different from anyone I've ever known. You intrigued me from the start, when I met you with Rob. Part of it was the boxing: I couldn't believe anyone would do that – if they had any intelligence at all. When I realized you are intelligent, I wanted to find out more. So, I insisted on seeing you box. I didn't know what to expect, really."

"So you saw, then what?"

"I was fascinated! You were so intent, so focused, and so brutal! I knew then I had to have you, come what may. Poor Rob."

"And now you have me, brutality and all."

"Strange thing, though. As I got to know you, I realized you may be the most sensitive man I've ever known."

"So, what am I, really?"

"A tender brute. How's that for an oxymoron?"

"But you do love me?"

"Yes, very much."

"That's all that matters."

"Strength and tenderness are an exciting combination," she sighed.

They drifted off to sleep, but in the wee hours she let him out and he walked to the Quad to catch a couple hours sleep. But he was restless, for he had but two days to recoup his fighting mood. He had never slighted training so close to a major competition before; however, he would have had it no other way. It had been the night of a lifetime!

He met the Gottis at the Y Sunday afternoon for a light workout. Don Gotti was rarin' to go, as was his father. Bauer tried to wax enthusiastic but was only modestly successful. Monday he jogged a couple miles, did "stretches" for a half-hour and shadowboxed three rounds. At four p.m. he did a live interview with the local radio station and learned the University was behind him "solidly," or so the interviewer said.

Monday evening he told Jan goodbye, lying with her on the bed without speaking for over an hour. "I love you," she said as he departed at nine o'clock.

"Thanks, Jan. I need that."

Tuesday morning he joined the Gottis at the railroad station and headed for Chicago. They arrived at the arena at mid-afternoon for weighing, hotel assignments and fight scheduling the next day. Don noted a sameness among all contestants: tension, bravado, insecurity. A recent tragedy did little to alleviate the mood.

Talk of the boxing world was the death of Sam Baroudie, who had been knocked senseless by hard-punching Lem Franklin on the previous night; Baroudie died shortly afterwards. Starkly, billboards at the arena entrance still featured posters hyping the Baroudie-Franklin fight, complete with posed pictures of both boxers. Although they had been pros, this nuance did little to alleviate concern among the Simon-pure amateurs now assembling.

Don reminded himself that this was nothing compared to the night before the Rapido River crossing in January 1944. He could handle this foreboding with eyes closed, literally. Actually he slept well Tuesday night.

Don Gotti went on at one p.m. and lost a sluggish fight by split decision. His father was furious at the outcome, blaming the train ride, accommodations and officiating. He accompanied Bauer to the ring fortified by several quick drinks to drown his disappointment. Don had the feeling Bob Gotti cared little one way or the other about the outcome of Bauer's match.

Don himself felt better after seeing his opponent, Gene Young from Rockford, Illinois. Young appeared intimidated, and Don did little to disabuse him. In the ring, however, Bauer couldn't follow through. He felt awkward, dull and lethargic throughout the first round. The second was little improved, with both fighters looking listless.

"You're even," Gotti told Don after two rounds. "Win this one and you win the fight."

Don got up from the stool early, breathed deeply to brace himself. He would go all out now. He moved smartly to center ring and snapped a couple jabs to Young's face. He jabbed once more and followed with a hard left hook. In doing so, Don left himself open for a straight right that came from nowhere. His trip to the canvas was an eerie experience.

Don floated weightlessly for an instant before his rump hit the deck. His head seemed perfectly clear, but he had no recollection of what had put him down. Don bounced to his feet to demonstrate it had been a fluke, a lucky punch. The referee looked into Bauer's eyes and then waved the match to continue. But something was not right.

"Hold on! Hold on!" Gotti was shouting from the corner.

"He thinks I'm hurt," Don mused.

He reflexively jabbed with his left as Young bore in, swinging both hands furiously. Don backed against the ropes and eventually tied up his shorter, stockier opponent. But Young sought to break clear and finish the fight. "Hold on! Hold on!" Gotti continued to shout. "How long before the bell?" Don wondered as the referee pushed them apart.

Young charged in again, but Don connected with a crisp left hook that startled his opponent. Don next unloaded a left jab and straight right to the face that shook Young. "You got him!" Gotti shouted. "Follow up!"

Don uncorked a left-right-left combination that staggered Young again and stirred the crowd. Knowing he had to deck his opponent to win, Don advanced with left jabs and solid rights to the head. Young was hanging on as the bell sounded.

Back in his corner, Gotti splashed Don's face with a cold, dripping sponge – unusual that! While massaging Bauer's neck vigorously, Gotti asked, "You all right?"

"I'm O.K.," Don insisted. "I'll get him this round."

"Fight's over, Don. You lost!"

Since it was only four p.m., Don wanted to catch a train for Iowa City that evening. He wanted out of Chicago as quickly as possible. He wanted to see Jan as quickly as possible; tomorrow was a long way off! But Bob Gotti would have none of it. "Stick around tonight and get a good night's sleep," he said. "Tomorrow we'll go back together."

Don walked off his "fuzziness" after showering. Then he sat with the Gottis through the evening fights. They went for a steak dinner, after which Don helped young Gotti put his drunken father to bed.

They caught the train at eleven-thirty a.m. and arrived in Iowa City at mid-afternoon. Bob Gotti suggested Don go to Student Health to be checked for a concussion. "He blasted you pretty good," Gotti said.

"Don't worry about it," Don replied. "I've been hit harder."

Don dropped his bag at the Quad and went to find Jan. Her Modern Dance class should have just ended, so he went to her house. When no one answered, he headed for Whetstone's. He swung by the dance studio on his way and saw Jan just entering the front door. He called to her – and drew attention from passing students.

When she saw Don, Jan rushed back and threw her arms about his waist. As he bent to kiss her, she scrutinized his face. "I heard you lost a 'furious' fight," she said.

"I'm fine, especially now. I wanted to come back yesterday, but Gotti wouldn't let me."

"A student's waiting," Jan explained, "but I'll see you at Whetstone's in an hour."

Don went directly to Whetstone's, where he drew stares as he entered. When he heard his name called, Don spotted a Daily Iowan reporter beckoning from a nearby table. Don accepted the reporter's invitation to be interviewed.

The peg was that Iowa University should have a boxing team, using Don and young Gotti who would enroll next fall as the nucleus. Since two of the Big Ten schools already had boxing teams, why not Iowa? Don didn't mention his own suspect collegiate eligibility, but supported the idea. If his prominence in the sport was useful in this respect, what was the harm?

Jan arrived as the interview ended. As a performer, she recognized the need for publicity, so she was pleased that Don would be featured. The reporter said a photographer would be at the next boxing workout to take pictures.

"I need sugar," Don told Jan, so they shared a banana split. He answered her questions about the fight and volunteered Gotti's suggestion that he see a doctor.

"Maybe you should," she said.

He dismissed her concern by saying, "Look at it this way, Jan. If they put me in the hospital for observation, I'll sleep alone tonight."

"And we wouldn't want that, would we?" she laughed.

After agreeing to meet later, Don returned to the Quad to get organized. Before tackling academics, he set about recovering physically. He jogged the track a couple times and stretched to ease out stiffness. He took a prolonged hot shower and felt much better afterwards.

They met at a student eatery where they had light fare. Then they went to Jan's. When they had disrobed, she examined the welts and bruises. He sought to ease her concern by saying, "That's normal for a fight like this one." She wouldn't be put off easily, though. "What about a concussion?" she asked.

He digressed by turning amorous, kissing and fondling her. After making love, when they should have been still mesmerized, she persisted in the discussion. He saw then that this had to be talked out.

"What is it, Jan?" he asked. "Do you want me to quit?"

"No, I want you to do what you want, especially something you excel at. And I'm proud you're a boxer, but I still don't fully understand your dogged persistence – if that's the right characterization."

"You have to know more about my background, my early life," Don explained. "After I joined the army, boxing helped me get ahead, get recognized. In one of those company-street impromptu boxing matches, I decked a guy bigger and stronger than me. After that, I boxed in 'smokers,' evening shows to entertain the troops. I usually won, which paid off in several ways. I was promoted ahead of others and people respected me. Those things happened because of boxing.

"Of course, when we went into combat, boxing stopped. But after Cassino in Italy we were pulled back to get ready for Anzio. While we waited for replacements to be mixed in with us old hands, boxing started up again because all it took was a set of gloves. I'd just turned twenty and had my full size and strength, finally. Now I could knock a man out with either hand and everyone loved that except for the guy who got knocked out!

"I usually won by a knockout, which made me a marked man. Then, too, I became a little cocky so I was heading for a fall. An ex-pro fighter sandbagged me. At first he toyed with me, then he started hitting hard and in combinations. He knocked me down several times, but I bloodied his nose and staggered him a couple times. Some enjoyed seeing me get smacked around, but they didn't see me counted out. In fact, the ex-pro was the one hanging on at the end!

"I walked around 'goofy' for a day or so after the fight, so Doc sent me back to be checked for concussion. But medics were busy treating combat casualties so they just 'observed' me. If I conked out, what was the big deal? Guys were being blown to bits every day. After a week or so, I wrangled my way out of there. Back with my unit at Anzio, I found my platoon had been pretty well wiped out again. So, in a perverse way, boxing probably saved my life.

"That, my dear, is behind my attitude. Then, too, if it weren't for boxing maybe you and I wouldn't be lying here together now."

"And that would have been too bad," Jan said pensively. "You're the best thing that ever happened to me."

"And you to me. By the way, when do we dance again?"

CHAPTER VII

DISTURBING SIGNS

After four semesters at Iowa University, Don Bauer knew he could earn a degree. He had righted himself after the disastrous first year and now had a solid C average. He had to make up a couple requirements, but he could do that in a summer. He was confident, too, that he could continue boxing and a part-time job as well. Although these activities cut into study time, they furnished diversion and money he needed.

Then there was Jan. Not only did she add spice, but her advice provided a sure azimuth. Had he not connected with her, Don probably would not still be on campus. Jan prompted him to consider summer school in 1947.

"You should raise your grade point," she urged. "Summer courses are a good way to do that while gaining credits you need."

Jan would not be in Iowa City most of the summer. However, she would be in nearby Atalissa with her family and Don could visit her there. He registered for Ed Psych and Government. Then Student Employment gave him a lead on a job that would pay a dollar an hour helping a craftsman remodel a local department store. Don was accepted and began his four-hour afternoon stints the following day.

Jan spent two weeks tidying up and bidding him goodbye. They went to Legion Hall on nights when a combo played danceable music. They would have a beer or two and dance ostentatiously to the delight of some and awe of others. Jan, of course, was the star as she did spins in a skirt that revealed a lot of leg. They bounced in the Lindy, and occasionally Jan would slide between his legs and return in an eye-popping display.

Their elan caused a stir, of course, but never really went astray. Because Jan was attractive and accomplished, men couldn't bring themselves to fault her and women wouldn't lest they appear envious. Then, too, the proprietor loved her show because it was good for business.

On warm evenings, they walked about town and campus. When the moon was up, they often took a blanket with them and joined other couples lying on the slopes overlooking Iowa River. The night before Jan left, they river-banked until midnight. He saw her off on the bus after coffee at Whetsone's the next morning.

A week later, Don boxed on a card arranged by Bob Gotti at the local softball diamond. Don Gotti was the featured fighter, of course, but Bauer appeared in the semi-windup. The good-sized crowd on hand gave him an enthusiastic reception, and he didn't disappoint the fans. Don started quickly and knocked out his opponent in a little over a minute of fighting.

"A lucky punch," he told the Daily Iowan reporter afterwards. "I'm glad because I didn't want another brawl like the one in Chicago!"

Although things were going well for Don Bauer, he was disturbed by a deteriorating international situation. An increasingly bellicose Soviet Union reminded Americans of the 1930s. Most disturbing was the intractability of Joseph Stalin in every United States' attempt to reach accommodation. Of course, Stalin had learned from Hitler about coercion and intimidation.

"An Iron Curtain is descending across Europe," Winston Churchill had warned the world back in 1946. Churchill, who had been right about Hitler's Nazis, now updated his assessment of Stalin's Communists: "I am convinced there is nothing they admire so much as strength." He was implying, of course, that western powers should get ready. Unlike the 1930s, Free World leaders were giving no thought to appeasement this time.

If the Soviets were to attack in Europe, no one would be untouched – not in an era of atomic bombs! Don was still just twenty-four years old and in good health. He would surely be recalled in a national emergency, so maybe his war-fighting years were not over. He kept these thoughts to himself, but found his sleep disturbed more frequently now.

Coincidentally, he read in the newspaper that Reserve Officers Training was coming back. ROTC had thrived at Iowa before the war, as it had in most land-grant colleges. However, it had been put in abeyance during the early 1940s when young men had gone off to war instead of college. Now a Professor of Military Science and Tactics, Colonel William J. Jackson, West Point 1917, was on campus to see that ROTC returned fully in September.

Don noted that voluntary senior ROTC—which veterans could join—would not only lead to commissioning in the reserves but would pay participants $27.90 a month. Combining that with the $75 – up from the original $50 – from the GI Bill would add up to $102.90 monthly. Don wanted to buy a car more than ever, so he now had more than passing interest in senior ROTC.

Don put $100 down on a new car that would be delivered when his name reached the top of a list, but he soon learned that his name would not move without a bribe. Next, he started looking for a good used car. But, then, this tack was fraught with hazards, too. Any used car was at least five years old and had had "the hell driven out of it." Still he looked and inquired.

He did get a break, however. A salesman at the Pontiac agency in Iowa City had been with Don during the war. After an exchange of war stories, this old buddy promised to keep his eye open for a trade-in by "a little old lady who never drove much." A few days later, Don was called about a possibility.

The prospective car, a 1940 Ford business coupe, had smooth tires, a corroded battery, and a broken odometer. But the salesman promised Don that it would be in tip-top shape and the price would be reasonable. Don put up earnest money and then he fretted that he had thrown it away.

When he picked up the car a few days later, Don was encouraged. Serviceable tires were on the ground, a new battery was in place and the odometer now worked. The repairman had arbitrarily put 50,000 miles on the odometer so people won't think it's a new car. Ha! Ha! The next weekend Don drove to Homesite and back and was convinced he had not made a bad deal, despite having paid twice what this model had cost new in 1940!

The summer passed quickly. Don received an A in Ed Psych and a B in Government. He now had a comfortable C+ grade point and was on schedule to graduate in June 1949. He also mended fences with an old friend.

He came face to face with Rob Stone on campus one day. Rob was his old self, acting as though nothing had ever come between them. He bought Don a coke and during the ensuing conversation insisted they play golf. Under the circumstances, and because his summer job had ended, Don agreed. He drove by in his car and picked up Rob, who had an extra set of golf clubs.

They played on a nine-hole course on the eastern edge of Iowa City. The course was not crowded, so Rob patiently instructed Don on the basics of driving a golf ball. Once away from the tee, Rob demonstrated what club, stance and approach should be used for each lie. He cautioned Don to not muscle the ball but to let the club and correct form do the work. They walked about the course on a pleasant afternoon and Don thoroughly enjoyed the outing. Afterward, he drove Rob back to West Branch.

Rob invited Don to stay for the supper Mrs. Stone had on the table. Since this was his second visit—he had been at the Stones for Thanksgiving Day in 1946—Don felt comfortable. He learned that the Stones had lost their other son in the war—killed in action shortly after D-Day in Normandy. But that wasn't the only bit of startling news Don was to garner that unusual day. After supper, Rob and Don went to the local bar for a beer. They commented on the facility and people present before Rob brought up a delicate matter. "How are you and Jan doing?" he asked matter-of-factly.

Don was taken aback but managed to say, "Fine."

"Jan's a fun girl," Rob continued as though everything was just fine with him.

"Sure is."

"She teach you to dance?"

"Yes."

"Jan really can dance."

"Yeah, she draws a crowd."

"I've known her since she was a girl," Rob continued. "Her family used to live here in West Branch. She tell you that?"

"No. She never mentions you."

"Even though I was older, we dated back in high school. She was a freshman, I was a senior and a good jock, if I say so myself. She was a cheerleader, of course, and always popular. She liked to roller-skate; she's good at that, too. She's like Sonja Henie on roller skates."

"I can believe that."

"During the war they moved away," Rob explained. "But we kept in touch, and when I came back we started to date again. So you see we go back a long way."

Don considered apologizing for having interfered, but Rob didn't really give him a chance. And Don was soon glad that he hadn't said what he had in mind. "No matter what's happened," Rob said, "We'll go on."

That little bombshell caught Don's attention.

"This has happened before," Rob explained. "She's gone off with other guys from time to time, but she always comes back to me. I can't really blame her. She has lots of chances. I'm sure you've noticed guys really fall for her."

Rob was so devoid of any trace of vindictiveness that Don was disarmed. He couldn't bring himself to protest, disagree, or even inquire further. There was yet another surprise! "I'm painting your picture," Rob announced. "Remember the photo in the paper after the Cedar Rapids fight? Well, I sketched it out and now I'm putting paint to it. I'll give it to you when I finish."

Don's uneasiness increased as Rob continued: "I'm not a serious art student. I just paint what I like, and boxing has always intrigued me. Your inviting Jan and me that night got me started." When Don dropped Rob off, they went inside and Don saw the painting in progress. He was impressed—and flattered. The painting was good, very good!

A very confused Don Bauer returned to Iowa City that night. Although incredulous of Rob's revelation, Don had to admit it had a certain plausibility. Perhaps Jan had taken him in, was just toying with him. But even if that were true, what should he do? Could he get along without her? Don was still concerned two days later when he journeyed to Atalissa.

Although somewhat subdued in front of her parents, Jan seemed happy to see Don. She noted that he was quieter than usual but thought maybe it was because he wanted to create a good impression with her parents. However, when he remained moody even when he took her to show off his car, she asked why.

"I talked to Rob," he replied.

She looked directly at him but waited.

"He said you've ditched him before but have always come back."

"That was before you," she replied calmly.

"So, when am I used up?"

Jan thought about the pointed question a moment, then answered indirectly.

"Rob and I have known each other since high school," she explained. "But you know how kids are. Frivolous and whimsical. When Rob left for the Navy, he asked me to wait for him. Caught up in the drama of the time, I said I would. When his brother was killed, I consoled his parents, and I gushed in letters to Rob. Surely, you understand that."

"In a way, yes."

"When Rob came back in debilitated condition, I spent a lot of time with him during recuperation. Then when he could be up and about, we did things together. That's when I taught him to dance and he taught me to roller skate. Every one was getting engaged, so when he asked I accepted. It bothered me, though, that I liked him but I wasn't sure I loved him. But that's why people get engaged, isn't it?"

"You slept with him?"

She studied Don's face as she answered. "Yes, we've been intimate. But that should not surprise you. You must have detected I was not a virgin."

"Were there others?"

"Only you."

Don had parked on the side of the country road at that point. He took her in his arms and kissed her, to let her know that he wanted to believe her. Shortly she drew away, for she had more to say.

"Don, I have feelings for you that I don't have for Rob. That's the difference. I ask myself what it is but I can't explain. I just accept it's intuitive, you're what I live for."

"Say no more," he said. "I'm the same way about you, so let's just keep it that way."

As they drove back, Jan sat very close and held his hand where it lay upon her thigh. During supper Don talked readily with Mr. Dallas, discussing the late war and Don's participation in boxing. He complimented Mrs. Dallas on her fine cooking. He sensed they liked him, whatever Rob's relationship may have meant to them. Later, he bid Jan farewell on the porch and departed believing the visit had gone well.

The next morning, Don drove to Homesite for Deborah's wedding in early September. He was immediately caught up in running errands and taking people for appointments. He met arrivals at the railroad station in Council Bluffs and helped them settle in at one place or another.

Don, Brad, and Frank were ushers at the late-morning wedding. A reception was held in the parish hall, followed by a sit-down dinner prepared by the church ladies. A bar was set up in the cloakroom with mixed drinks to order. Payment was by voluntary contributions to a kitty, which was passed on to the bride and groom.

Don sat across from an attractive young lady during dinner. She was with a young man named Dale, who seemed more attentive to a girl on his other side. When the band struck up <u>String of Pearls</u>, Don asked the girl opposite to dance.

Although her escort nodded, he muttered, "The next one's mine, though."

"I'm Ella," the girl announced as they walked to the dance floor.

"And I'm Don."

"I know. I've heard about you."

Ella was a good dancer. Not a Jan, of course, but better than most. She followed Don's Lindy routines with zesty moves and seemed to enjoy the attention they garnered. As they returned to the table, Ella murmured, "Ask again."

Don danced with Deborah and others, but he still favored light-hearted Jeanne who adjusted readily to style changes. Perceptive, too, was Jeanne. She warned Don that Ella's date was jealous! "I'll give him no grief," Don promised.

However, when a Waltz started and few took to the floor, Don glanced at Ella. As she got up to join him, the look on her escort's face was unmistakable. That Ella and Don sparkled on the floor only added to the animosity. Upon returning to the table, Don thanked Ella's date and decided to butt out. Later, when Ella scribbled her phone number on a napkin and slipped it to Don, he tucked it away knowing he would not follow up.

Don had been reminded again how far out of touch he was here. Earlier, Uncle Walt, an affluent farmer, had told Don he was wasting his time boxing and going to college. Don brushed aside the gratuitous remark by asking if Uncle Walt had something better to offer.

"You can go to work for me by the month," Uncle Walt had responded. "But I'm sure that's not good enough for you. You want the moon!"

"Maybe so," Don retorted, "but look at it this way. If I shoot for the moon and miss, at least I'll end up among the stars!"

The riposte drew laughter from those privy to the discussion and a parting shot from Uncle Walt: "Spoken like a true dreamer, my boy!"

Truthfully, Don didn't much care. Other than his immediate family, little in Homesite appealed to him anymore. He couldn't understand how Homesiters could settle for so little. Take the case of Deborah and Paul. They would return from a brief wedding trip and tend to fall harvesting. Over the years, they would be frugal, successful, raise a family, and settle for contentment. That was it!

But sometimes things didn't work out so well. Take Frank, for example. He worked hard, but working for Dad wasn't paying off. They didn't have the assets, acreage and good soil, so Frank hired out to other farmers to increase his income, but daily wages would not suffice now that a baby had arrived. Therefore, Frank's wife was casting her gaze southward, to her home in Missouri where prospects seemed better. So Frank said he may be "cutting out," a move that would devastate Dad.

Brad, too, was struggling. He had been released by the Cardinals, who were looking at younger players. Brad now realized his age handicap would be difficult to overcome. Still, he would give baseball one more try.

"I've signed on with an independent team in western Texas," he announced. "If I don't make it there, I'll see you in Iowa City."

Even Jeanne had lowered her sights. When Don asked if she would go to college, she replied, "No thanks. High school is all the education I want." Her outlook had changed once she started going steady with a classmate, Verne Meckley. Now she would follow a path similar to Deborah's.

Yet, in a way Don envied them. In small Iowa towns things are simple, manageable, predictable. Crops, kids, and a comfortable home usually are enough. Homesite—or a place like it—is all people needed. "But if vision stops at the horizon," he wondered, "how can one see the stars?"

So Don Bauer returned to Iowa City in the fall of 1947 a bit of a pariah. He moved back into his old room in the Quad with Ed Banyon. He took a job for two meals a day in the Quad Cafeteria, which had the advantages of better meals and working at "home." Jan, too, continued living with Aunt Becky, so everything was as before. Shortly, Don Bauer was to embark on a course that would have been unthinkable two years earlier.

During registration Don introduced himself to Colonel Jackson, who beamed when Don said he was a veteran considering senior ROTC.

"Others have already signed up," Colonel Jackson replied. "I'm confident we'll have a full complement this year."

So Don signed on, too.

The decision had taken on a life of its own. Once Don had concluded that conflict with the Soviet Union was in the offing, he began preparing. He discussed the matter with Jan, who agreed that ROTC would be a prudent step, and she didn't seem at all alarmed at the prospect. "It doesn't seem fair that you should go again," she said, "but it would be better to be an officer this time, I'm sure."

Discussion concerning the future was rare in their relationship. Even though talk of marriage never came up, conversations always assumed they would be together in some arrangement still to unfold. Typically, during the ROTC exchange Jan had said, "I'll go along with your choice, as long as it includes me!" So they went on, taking each eventful day as it came and went.

When next they went to Legion Hall, Rob Stone was there. Don saw him standing at the bar as they entered, but Jan appeared not to notice. Don debated whether or not to ask Rob over; however, Rob resolved the dilemma by abruptly departing without even a glance in their direction. Relieved of what would have been an awkward presence, Don and Jan soon immersed themselves in dancing.

Don now was doing well academically. He could analyze readings and lectures and boil them down to essentials. He could memorize when he had to. And he could write coherent and substantive reports. He wondered now why he had been so intimidated at the beginning.

Obviously, Don Bauer had attained academic status when Smoky Blair asked him to save a seat for Jim Blount during a School Health test. Smoky was the varsity basketball star and the most spectacular player in the Big Ten Conference, if not the country. Blount, star pitcher on the baseball team and a major league prospect, was having difficulty with the details of a course that dealt with communicable diseases. Bauer was not in the varsity clique, per se, but he understood jock jargon well enough.

The transaction required nothing overt from him. Blount, waiting outside the classroom, followed Don to a seat from which Blount could pick off an answer here and there, much as he would pick off a base runner without really looking. Of course, Blount was well practiced in the move and aroused no suspicions on the part of the test administrator.

Bauer had prepared himself well and listed details for diphtheria, small pox, measles, chicken pox, and so forth. Then he spent time checking back over the answers. When Blount grunted "that's it," Don turned in his paper.

When test results were posted, Bauer received an A-minus and Blount a C-plus. The discrepancy was reconciled when Blount confessed he had guessed at a few to keep things "honest." A side bar was that varsity lettermen were friendlier toward Bauer after that, especially when the Hawkeyes had a winning season in baseball.

Because of his military experience, Bauer excelled in ROTC. He was familiar with small-unit tactics, geography, and history. He was proficient in Close Order Drill and marched his platoon of beginners to and fro under the approving eye of a faculty sergeant. And sure enough, a check for $27.90 arrived each month.

Other aspects were also pleasant. Don had thought he might be heckled when he wore the ROTC uniform about campus on drill days; however, he encountered nothing untoward. If anything, student reaction was favorable. Any latent student cynicism was no doubt curbed by ominous signals from overseas. After all, less than a decade had passed since Hitler and Tojo turned the world on its ear.

Comradery quickly developed among veterans in ROTC. Cadets would congregate before and after drill sessions to banter and reminisce. War stories abounded, of course, but sobering remarks on the Soviet Union's hostility were a part as well.

Some changes were made in boxing that fall. Young Gotti had been drafted into the Army during the summer, so he was out of the picture. However, his dad continued to train Bauer and a lightweight and a welterweight who had been added to Gotti's stable of club fighters. Henceforth, they would no longer focus on amateur shows but would fight openly for money—more or less.

Don's first match was in Rock Island, Illinois, against a Negro middleweight named Mason Lee. Lee was built like a reed, tall and slender, but he hit like a sledgehammer, according to Gotti. This semifinal fight would pay Don $40, win or lose. Against the tall, hard-hitting Lee, Don took the classic boxer-puncher approach. He jabbed with his left and tied up the charging Lee, who would paw with his left twice and then uncork a wild right from somewhere near the floor. Most of the time he missed, other times he hit low. Such failings did not deter Lee in the slightest: One punch would do it! Of course, the officials penalized Lee for his wildness.

"Close, but you won the round," Gotti opined after the first round. "Now test his jaw."

The first minute of the next round was a continuation of the first.

But when Lee pawed twice, Don slipped right and uncorked a crisp left hook to the jaw. He beat Lee's long uppercut by an instant and the tall man dipped to one knee where he knelt for a nine count. Lee shook his head a couple times and fell into a clinch. Thinking Lee might be feigning injury, Don jabbed repeatedly and waited for him to lead out once more. The crowd wanted a knockout and quickly grew impatient. When booing started, the referee urged both boxers to mix it up. But Lee would have none of it and the round ended on that note.

"He's whipped!" Gotti shouted in the corner. "Drop him again and it's all over."

Gotti was wrong. Lee was still intent on winning in the last round. With his head cleared and strength restored, Lee unleashed both hands in a furious assault. He pummeled Don's groin, hip and back with thudding blows. The referee warned Lee repeatedly about low punching but did little else to curtail the mayhem. Although Bauer never regained control of the fight, he won a unanimous decision because of the knockdown. Still, Don had absorbed a beating to his lower body.

"Look at it this way," Gotti said wryly afterwards. "Your face ain't marked."

Don took a break from boxing after that although he continued roadwork and calisthenics. He wanted to spend more time with Jan and dancing, but he was in for a surprise. The fun part of dance lessons was over. Jan, the perfectionist, now emphasized styling. Don recognized the importance of style in performance, but he did not enjoy this aspect at all. He preferred being natural so that he could throw himself into the rhythm and routine. Inevitably, Jan's insistence on more formality – and his reluctance in achieving it – caused tension at times.

"I dance for enjoyment," he would remind her.

"But you must do it right!" she would insist.

He usually went along, but it dawned on him eventually that she was pointing toward serious competition. This realization was intimidating because Don had no background in music – he couldn't always pick up the downbeat – he tended to carry his left shoulder high due to overdeveloped musculature from boxing, and he experienced difficulty in maintaining balance in precise movements.

"For what you have in mind, I'll always come up short," he warned her in a moment of candor. "I love to dance with you, to show you off, but I'll never be Fred Astaire!"

"How can you give up so readily?" she remonstrated. "We complement each other perfectly, but you must smooth out rough spots."

And so he would try again, reassured not so much by his progress but by her tenacity. Surely, her desire to continue stemmed from her love of him. Still, her ambition that could not be satisfied in Iowa City or by him seemed threatening.

Disturbing, too, was another perception of his. Jan seemed less enthusiastic about his boxing and even questioned his continuing the sport. Perhaps this was behind her emphasis on his dancing well. When he reminded her once more that boxing had helped bring them together, she unsettled him further by saying, "Perhaps we've moved beyond that point. Everything has a time and place, you know."

"I'll quit one day," he assured her.

"When will that be?"

"When the fascination is gone."

"Fascination?"

"Yeah, the ups and downs."

"What are you saying?"

"The 'down' is before the match. Every doubt I've ever had wells up in the dressing room. I won't do well! I might get hurt! I'm a psycho lump at that stage. I shut everything out – even you!"

Noting her attentiveness, Don went on.

"The 'up' starts when Gotti says, 'Let's go!' I pull myself together then. My heart thumps during the referee's instructions. When the bell finally rings I'm in charge. I can jab the guy to death, I can punch him out! But whatever, I win because I'm over the dread!"

She pondered his explanation a while, then commented: "I understand what you say. I've had similar emotions in music and dancing, even to the matter of dreading a performance. But not pain! I can't accept the pain part."

"Pain?"

"Yes, the blows, the bruises, the physical beatings."

"These things are just scores," he reminded her. "Points to mark up on one side or another. A punch is like a single in baseball. A knockout is like a home run the pitcher watches sail over the wall. So pain is disappointment, that's all it is."

"Don, I've seen the bruises, soothed them when you could barely stand the touch of my fingers. Even worse are 'hidden bruises,' the concussions that surely occur. What about them?"

"I never notice," he said dismissively.

"You suppress them, shut them out," she insisted. "I've noticed that your hearing's been affected. You do not hear high notes nor do you discern differences in musical pitch. And because of balancing difficulty you cannot hesitate while dancing."

"Shells and explosions ruined my hearing," he rationalized. "And I have flat feet from long marches under heavy loads, but it's not from boxing. I shake off punches like raindrops. I've never been knocked out and the only time I've been dazed was in high school."

"In high school?"

"A bigger kid teed off on me. Hit me a hell of a shot during a fuss in basketball. I walked around in a daze for hours, but I never passed out. Maybe that's why I turned to boxing – I never wanted to go through that again. And I haven't. I seldom get hit solidly, I'm good at slipping punches."

"You're very good at boxing," she said. "It's thrilling to witness your skills, but I don't want anything to happen to you. Please understand that."

The discussion ended then – for the time being.

Gotti landed a main event for Don in Oskaloosa, Iowa, shortly thereafter. He would be paid $50 to fight the local champion who had gone to the finals in national Golden Gloves last year. It would be a five-round match, so Don had to prepare himself for the longer fight. But increased training did not set well with Jan.

She had been grooming him for the Margot Rusel Open House in March, when the dance studio would open its doors in a three-hour promotion that featured demonstrations by instructors. Refreshments were included and the final hour would be open to free lessons for attendees. Of course, Jan would be spotlighted several times and she was assembling a wardrobe appropriate to each appearance. She wanted Don to dance with her as proof of her teaching methods.

They finally resolved the dispute after the University Prom in late February. The Tex Beneke orchestra played before an optimal attendance: enough couples to fill the floor, not so many as to crowd the dancers. Jan wore a low-cut clinging white formal that accented her lithe figure and amplified her natural flair. Don even bought a new suit for the occasion, and he managed to stay over his feet during the Rumba, Waltz, Cha-Cha, Samba, and Lindy. Jan took the opportunity to remind Don that style lessons were paying off.

Later, they went to the Jefferson Hotel Lounge for dessert. It seemed everyone there knew either Jan or Don, so a merry exchange of greetings buoyed both. Also, Jan told Don that her aunt would be out of town and they could go to her place afterwards.

Their lovemaking was a fervent communication, undoubtedly inspired by recent stresses. Throughout, they vowed and reassured one another that their relationship would never end. In the afterglow, she told Don not to be bothered by what Rob had said.

"I'll never leave you," she murmured.

"You can't ditch me, Jan," he cautioned. "For it's written in the heavens, believe me!"

"And in the forests, the mountains, and the winds!" she added.

They achieved accommodation on a more mundane level as well. He would train for his match as never before and she would perform with Billy Mickles, the male instructor. Furthermore, each would attend the other's event.

Don's boxing match took place three days before the Open House, which meant Jan would miss a rehearsal. She convinced Margot that she would be ready and that there was no alternative! Even Margot agreed at that point that Jan should go.

So Jan and Don drove the seventy-five miles to Oskaloosa on fight day, and arrived just before weighing in at four p.m. The card was a mixture of boxing and professional wrestling presented in a huge barn-like arena at the fair grounds. Boxing would start at six-thirty, so Don could expect to box about an hour later.

They went to a local restaurant for supper. Jan had a salad and Don a steak, baked potato and hot tea. Even though he tried to suppress his nervousness, his somber mood bothered her. She held his hand to reassure him but was further disturbed by tautness and coolness in his touch. Even the usual warmth in his gaze ebbed as he gathered himself for the contest ahead.

Next they walked about town, which alleviated the strain somewhat. They were back at the fairgrounds at six o'clock and looked over the interior of the building filled with chairs spaced around a raised ring at center. Don arranged with the promoter for Jan to sit a few rows back, near the aisle. Already fans were noisily entering the arena, so Don did not tarry long before heading for the dressing room.

Jan observed the proceedings with mixed emotions. She wanted to be positive because this involved someone she loved; however, the scene begged comparison to the refined settings at dance and music performances she was accustomed to. She told herself that this, too, was part of American culture and she should know about it. She was encouraged somewhat by the large number of women present but was taken aback by their boisterous behavior.

Don Bauer felt ill at ease as well. The wrestling teams–two women and two men–sat in the corner of the dressing room joking and smoking. When they began to dress for their ring appearances, Don noted the women slipped into togs without revealing any flesh. The men, on the other hand, didn't care. They removed trousers and pulled tights over exposed buttocks without a second thought.

Gotti arrived as Don was wrapping and taping his hands. Next, he shadowboxed to loosen up. The drill intrigued the female wrestlers, who watched with undisguised mischief.

"Stay away from me, honey," one cautioned. "I'd hate to have to put you on your back right here. Later will be O.K., though."

"Yeah," the other said. "He's cute!"

"Watch out for his jab, though," one of the men teased.

"Hey, I love a good jabber!" the first woman shot back.

"All right, you guys," Gotti interjected. "You're distracting him!"

"That's what I had in mind all along, honey," she replied. "Hey! You're kinda cute yourself."

Gotti seemed pleased. "They're professionals," he said to Don. "They put on a show every night. Tougher'n hell, those babes."

The promoter opened the door and announced "ready!" Gotti helped Don into his robe and they started for the ring. Don looked straight ahead as he passed within a few feet of where Jan sat, but she observed him closely.

Recalling his earlier revelations, she assumed he was now ready to go, to win big! As for herself, Jan would settle for the fight ending as humanely as possible. She wanted him to succeed, of course, but wondered if winning was really in their best interest. She was then distracted by the arrival in the ring of Don's opponent.

Bryce Jones was a hometown boy and clearly the crowd favorite. He was shorter than Don Bauer but stockier of build. In fact, Jan thought he looked more formidable because of his rugged features and heavier musculature. She guessed he might not be too bright, but that shouldn't be a handicap in such a brutal sport.

At ring center for the referee's instructions, both fighters sought to stare down the other with little success. Both returned to respective corners and loosened up, dancing about and swinging punches at imaginary foes. Crowd noise built impressively just before the bell rang. Jan became aware of her own heartbeats as the two men turned to face each other.

Don struck first, sending two quick jabs to Jones' face. He danced back, however, and countered with a looping left hook followed by a straight right to Don's jaw. Bauer sagged momentarily and the crowd roared. Hometowners wanted a knockout and quick!

Bauer shook off the blows and jabbed back. When Jones tried a left-right combination, Don moved inside and punched sharply to the belly. As they clinched, Bauer sensed he had scored well, so he waded in following the break and rocked his man with a crisp left hook. He followed with left jabs and a straight right that sent Jones reeling. Groans of disappointment emanated from Oskaloosa fans.

But Jones, egged on by the crowd, came back strong. He unloaded a combination of punches that Bauer struggled to stave off. And as the round drew to a close, Jones stepped up the pace, pummeling Bauer with a flurry of short punches that impressed the crowd and judges. Bryce Jones was savvy all right.

Jan was in awe, spellbound by blows dealt by first one fighter then the other. She had to admit to a fascination as she watched two trained boxers wreak havoc upon one another. Yes, indeed, there was an "up" involved, well evidenced by delirious fans all around.

She studied Don as he rested between rounds. He appeared confident despite having been bested at round's end. He listened attentively to Gotti's instructions. He bounded up at the last instant as Gotti inserted the mouthpiece.

Bryce Jones had stood during the break. Apparently, he believed he was stronger than his opponent and that he could end the fight early. Eagerly, he darted across the ring to meet Don just coming out of his corner at the bell.

Jones continued at a torrid pace. He fired combination after combination of punches, only to dance afterwards in taunting fashion. The crowd loved it!

When Don responded tentatively, Jan feared he was about to be knocked out. She saw his knees buckle several times, but somehow he never lost his poise. When Jones let up to catch his breath, Bauer again peppered away with left jabs. Steadily, he kept Jones off balance and frustrated him by being one move ahead of heavier blows.

Jan moved with the crowd, standing when others stood and sitting when they sat but she didn't raise her voice. Instead, she crossed her fingers and prayed, even when the more vociferous around her were calling for Jones to "knock him out!" One woman even called for Jones "to kill him!" which struck Jan as being extreme.

Slowly, Jones' strategy shifted. Rather than punch himself out, he appeared to be waiting for a clean shot that would end the fight. Of course, this pace favored Don, who now took charge. He jabbed away repeatedly, patiently and lulled Jones into believing the round would end this way. But when the referee pushed them apart after a clinch, Bauer stepped in and dropped Jones to one knee with a sharp left hook to the jaw.

Jones jumped back up as the count started and the bell rang – but he had been decked! Fans were stunned into silence, unwilling to believe their eyes. Only one shrill voice carried throughout that crowded arena: "Touche!" Jan called out to the dismay of those around her.

"You got their attention!" Gotti told Don. "Now hit him again."

The pace of round three moderated as both fighters accepted they might go the distance. Don boxed away, scoring points against his shorter foe and drawing a trickle of blood from Jones' nose. Even Jones' flurry at the end didn't change the outcome and Don won the round clearly.

"He's still ahead," Gotti surmised in the corner. "Keep pecking away and try to drop him again. That should do it."

Don stood and breathed deeply – and succumbed to the forbidden: He glanced in Jan's direction! Their eyes met and he was reminded of that match in Cedar Rapids when they first connected. Abruptly, the bell brought him back to Oskaloosa and the boxing ring.

Jones again came on strong in the fourth, moving constantly and firing crisp punches from all angles. On occasion he slipped Don's tormenting left jab and moved inside to bang away with both hands. It was not a good round for Bauer, who couldn't match his opponent's energy at that point.

Feeling drained, Don went into survival mode. He jabbed away at his darting target and drew encouragement when Jones' nose began to bleed again and a slit appeared above his left eye. Jones, too, noticed the bleeding and appeared disturbed as he returned to his corner when the round ended. Still, he had won the round and was comfortably ahead.

"You'll have to knock him out to win," Gotti said summarily during the break.

Bauer took full advantage of the minute's rest. The cool, wet sponge felt good against his benumbed face. He swigged from the water bottle, slushed the liquid in his mouth and spit it out. As the bell rang, he stood, accepted the mouthpiece, and felt somewhat rejuvenated.

Jones was unrelenting. He bobbed in and out and landed short, telling blows on his taller opponent. Bauer retaliated by going for the head with a vengeance, trying to land a crushing blow that would take Jones out or worsen his injuries. They took turns rocking each other with bombs as the fight approached its climax. Fans "oohed" and "aahed" as first one and then the other nearly went down. Jan closed her eyes and prayed for the bell to end the brutality.

With mere seconds to go, Bauer rocked Jones with a left hook to the jaw. The stricken fighter lunged forward in an effort to tie up Don and they met head on – literally! Bauer shook off a shower of bright flashes and saw blood gushing from Jones' forehead. The referee waved Bauer back and stopped the fight. All was confusion at the bell.

"You won!" Gotti shouted. "You TKO'd him!"

Fans conversed noisily as the referee and judges conferred. A doctor tended Jones' laceration while both managers shouted advice at officials. When Jones' manager returned to his fighter and Gotti continued to argue, Bauer knew the outcome. The bell rang for attention.

The announcer explained the rationale behind the decision. Although the referee had stopped the fight, not enough time remained for a ten count. Therefore, the judges' vote would obtain. Bryce Jones was declared winner by split decision!

Don congratulated Jones in his corner as the doctor continued stitching a nasty gash.

"Thanks," Jones growled. "We'll have to do it again some time."

"Sure. Why not?"

Don next found Jan, who kissed his cheek as he held her. A nearby fan patted Don's shoulder and said, "You were robbed!"

"The hell he was!" another shouted.

"Let's get out of here," Jan pleaded.

On their way to the dressing room, Don asked Jan what she thought of the outcome. "Let me just say you're a winner!" she replied with a squeeze of his hand.

Don quickly showered, picked up his $50, and they headed back to Iowa City. His eyes were puffed and a trace of blood oozed from a damaged nose, but overall Don felt good, even exhilarated. They stopped at a restaurant for apple pie a la mode and coffee and then traveled up the quiet highway. With Jan snuggled alongside, he drove with one hand; the other nestled in the warmth of her lap.

"Too bad you can't stay with me tonight," she said when they arrived at her aunt's house. "Maybe tomorrow night."

"That would be nice," he replied, feeling that he was indeed a winner.

Of course, ecstasy is perishable. Three days later Don Bauer felt regretful and a bit jealous at the Open House. Billy Mickles was a superb dancer who showed off Jan with a flair Don could never match. That Bauer would have handicapped the woman he loved was unsettling. The longer he witnessed the performance, the more insecure he became.

Slender, light of foot, and exquisitely groomed, Mickles was in his element. A loose-fitting shirt flattered his upper torso while tight-fitting trousers accentuated his nimbleness afoot. His posture was classic and style impeccable. The only flaw in Don's estimation was that Mickles appeared somewhat effeminate, hardly a shortcoming in the art of dancing.

Billy and Jan danced perfectly as a twosome, never missing a beat or muffing a turn. Mickles led Jan through an exotic Tango, an erotic Rumba, and a soaring Waltz. They were clearly the most spectacular pair there, and their dash and skill drew raves throughout and prolonged applause at the finish.

Don was reluctant to take to the floor during the free session that followed. Defensively, he told Jan that he would only make her look bad. Mischievously, she placed his right hand at her waist, held his left in a pose, and counted out the downbeat. Soon they were grooving away in the Lindy. When a Foxtrot followed, she moved to closed position, tilted her head upward and brushed his lips with a kiss.

"Now you know how deflated I felt in Oskaloosa," she said. "Maybe I was more so because you have danced with me but I have never boxed with you."

Not able to resist her mirth, he smiled, drew her close and whispered, "But we have wrestled quite a bit."

Restoring his confidence was not quite that simple, however, and Don never felt quite the same about dancing thereafter. Then, too, the realization that she was just launching her dancing career while he was winding up his boxing fling gnawed at him. Would he henceforth feel inadequate around her? Was this the first step in their drifting apart?

He was briefly distracted by a note from Libby Bowman in early May. She would be in town the following week and would like to see him if at all possible. She included a phone number and a date to call after her arrival from Evanston.

When he called she answered and gave him an address on Burlington Street where she was staying. Libby was sitting on the porch when he drove up, so he sat with her and they talked about the intervening months.

At the time she wrote the earlier note to Don, Libby was slipping into acute depression. Eventually she was hospitalized, given shock treatments and prolonged therapy. For more than a year she struggled to regain stability. She had thought about writing to him again but couldn't accomplish the task. Although now recovered, she was still confused about Don. Perhaps he could help her come to terms with this phase of her life.

Don was moved, of course, but he responded forthrightly. He told her how disappointed he had been after visiting her in Evanston that fateful spring. But he had gotten over it and finally worked out an academic goal. Then he had met Jan Dallas, who provided the passion and support he needed. When Libby asked if he loved Jan, Don said, "Yes, very much. We mean an awful lot to each other."

She nodded when he finished and said, "I'm happy for you."

"And you?" he asked. "What about the Mentor?"

"He transferred to an Ivy League college just before I wrote that letter to you," she replied. "His departure ended our relationship and precipitated my illness. I needed someone desperately. That's why I wrote to you."

"But you never followed up," he reminded her.

"I left you dangling, I know, but I had gone under by then. As I told you, I did start several times but couldn't finish a note to you. I hope you understand."

"I do," he assured her, and then asked, "What adventures are you into now?"

Libby smiled wanly and replied, "I don't do 'adventures' any more. I'm back in grad school, though, and should have my Masters in psychology next summer. I'm a better student now; after all, I've had firsthand experience, haven't I?"

He patted her hand and stood up to leave. When she arose and turned his way, Don put his arms around her. Libby leaned back to observe his face. Tenderly, she ran her fingers across his brow and down the bridge of his nose. "You have more marks now than way back then," she said softly.

"Yes, I know."

CHAPTER VIII

SOMBER REFLECTIONS

Don Bauer did not tell Jan Dallas about Libby Bowman. In his judgement, doing so would serve no useful purpose. Neither did Jan Dallas tell Don Bauer about Rob Stone. In her view, doing so would only upset him. But there was a difference between the two omissions: Don Bauer had bid Libby Bowman farewell.

Of course, Don heedlessly contributed to building tensions. When he told Jan he would be going to ROTC summer camp at Fort Riley, Kansas, she was disappointed. Then when he told her he would be gone for eight weeks – the third week in June till the second week in August – she was stunned.

"Why, you'll be gone all summer," she scolded.

"Maybe we can meet in Kansas City at the halfway mark," he suggested.

"It all depends," she sniffed. "I'm not sure what I'll be doing at that point."

Realizing she had not been prepared, Don explained that summer camp was part of senior ROTC that she had agreed to. But his point was not well taken.

"You said there'd be a training camp," she rejoined, "but I thought maybe a week or so at the most."

"Sorry I misled you, but I can't do anything now. We'll have to work it out."

Her pique cast a pall over the semester's ending, so he put off leaving Iowa City till the last day possible in order to shorten their separation. They danced, river-banked, romanced, and did all the things they had always enjoyed, but a taint remained.

Jan's aunt was out of town their last night together, so Don stayed over. Although Jan was accommodative in most respects, he sensed less ardor and spontaneity when they made love.

"What's wrong?" he asked.

"The illusion's shattered, Don. The bubble has burst."

"You still love me?"

"Yes, but I'm not secure anymore. If our relationship is to end, maybe this is the start."

"Why even say that?"

"This summer is pivotal," she continued. "We must start thinking about graduation next year. Then what?"

"We'll work out something."

"For example?"

"We have a year to cross that bridge, so why quarrel now?"

"But have you thought about it at all?"

"Some," he replied tentatively.

"How so?"

"Well, we know boxing's out. I thought maybe ROTC might lead to something, but you don't like that now. I could coach in high school, but I'm weak in major sports. So I'll come up with something else."

"And perhaps you will," she said patronizingly.

"In a way, Jan, you've been rough on me."

"I have?"

"Yes. It's bad enough that you don't like what I do, but when I think of your dancing professionally it gets worse. You'll go off to Chicago or New York and leave me behind. That's not reassuring, believe me."

"But you can go too. That's why I've worked with you."

"That won't do it, Jan. Not in a hundred years!"

"And why not?"

"It's all that 'queer' stuff you'd have me do."

"Queer stuff?"

"Yeah, you want me to act like Billy Mickles."

"Never! I don't want you to lose your masculinity – ever!"

Her stout protest seemed to exorcise a demon and they melded together naturally. He marveled at how well they fit. As she lay with her arm and leg draped across his naked body, Jan began tracing tiny circles on his chest with a finger as she talked on. "I need closeness," she murmured. "I don't know what I'll do when you're not here."

"The summer'll fly by," he promised, "and I'll have things worked out then."

She lay without speaking for the longest time, sorting her thoughts.

"Don."

"Yes?"

"What if we're star-crossed?"

"What do you mean?"

"Supposing Polaris is obscured. What if clouds blot out the North Star? How will you find your way back then?"

"But it won't happen! You see Polaris is unfailing!"

"I wish I could be as confident."

"Jan, how can you not believe? What were the odds against our meeting? Yet, all those twists and turns in our lives occurred precisely so that at the appointed time and place our azimuths intersected. It was meant to be! Otherwise, our lives would've been pointless."

"I want to believe," she said and snuggled closer.

They slept then, throughout the foreshortened night. The next morning she fixed breakfast before he departed. Without a doubt, their differences had been reconciled and he departed in an optimistic mood.

Don stayed overnight in Homesite. News there was mixed. Deborah and Paul had had a good farming year and were now expecting a baby in August. Jeanne was still going steady with her classmate and seemed content. Brad was back after being released once more from a minor league team, but his reappearance was timely. He could help Dad with the farm work, while pitching for independent teams throughout the state for pay. He was still considering going to Iowa University, but didn't know if he could make first semester this year.

Frank, indeed, had gone south, so Brad was filling in. Frank, his wife, and baby girl had moved back to her family's neighborhood where he would be a day laborer until moving on to a farm the following spring. Dad was broken up, of course, but Mom was philosophical. She'd had a similar experience early in her marriage.

"It never works out for the woman," Mom said. "And when the wife's unhappy the husband's going to be unhappy. She'll see to that!"

Don was thankful he had missed the breakup, and that he would stay just one night in Homesite. After all, things were settling down. Crop prospects were good and Brad and Dad were shopping for a car. So, Don moved on to Fort Riley after promising to stop again when he returned in August.

Before leaving, however, he called Jan in Atalissa. She was happy to hear from him and said she was looking forward to Kansas City whenever he set a time. She even said she would like to meet Mom and Dad next fall, another indication she was thinking positively.

Don reached Fort Riley at noon and followed markers to Camp

Funston. Reception there was as familiar as yesterday. He signed in, drew bedding and fatigues from the supply room, and staked out a cot in an all-too-familiar squad room of the World War II barracks. Next, he went for lunch in the mess hall at the end of the company street.

At 1400 hours (two p.m.) he joined other cadets for the first briefing. Instructions were repetitive, but meeting the cadre officers and NCOs assembled from the various college ROTC faculties and fellow ROTC cadets was beneficial. The day closed with an hour of dismounted drill under cadre supervision. After supper Don joined other cadets for a beer at the PX branch. Taps sounded across the forlorn Kansas countryside at 2300 hours (eleven p.m.) to complete Don's homecoming.

Cadets finished orientation the next day, Saturday, in an auditorium. Then they drew and cleaned weapons, marched in formation under orders from randomly selected cadets, and picked up schedules and material for Monday classes. A notice on the bulletin board provided unit assignments and weekend details. Don was a squad leader and on guard Saturday night. Since he didn't get off guard duty until noon on Sunday, it was a short weekend for him.

Training began early Monday. After breakfast, cadets were inspected in ranks and all failed. Then they were inspected in squad rooms and again all failed. However, most recognized these failures were preordained in order to establish standards for the ensuing weeks. Veterans recalled this as an old Army trick, so they were tempted to believe nothing was new about ROTC summer camp. But there was a subtle distinction: Cadets were to keep in mind they were being trained as commissioned officers, a focus that made all the difference in the world. As Don repeated basic training in dismounted drill, marksmanship, and small-unit tactics, he thought not so much of his own proficiency but that of those he would lead. And the horizon was elevated now as well. Lowly tasks would be regarded as rungs up the ladder to battalion, regiment, division and beyond!

In pondering commissioned service, Don concluded responsibility was fundamental. But he soon found that responsibility was insidious: It permeated every task, thought, and action. So this changed perspective motivated him and other cadets now. The men, the mission, and the unit would dictate his behavior as an officer.

Planners had taken this into account in designing summer training, of course. Cadets were scored on how well they marched, fired a weapon, read a map, and solved problems, but they were evaluated on how well they led and supervised. Thus, cadets rotated throughout leadership positions during the eight weeks at camp.

Overall, Don Bauer fared well. He fired expert with the M-1 rifle, carbine, and most crew-served weapons. He excelled at map reading and using the lensatic compass. (Polaris was alive and well!) After squad leader, he became platoon sergeant, platoon leader, and then company commander during the culminating tactical exercises. True, his men were fellow cadets – not the usual enlisted men – but Bauer led and controlled without mishap.

He also starred off-duty when they competed in athletics. Cadets fought fiercely for pride and unit standings. Don played on winning softball, baseball and volleyball teams, and placed third in the mile run. Of course, competitions extended beyond playing fields in the PX beer hall where comradery flourished during rehashing and hassling.

Don Bauer came up with a theory on the benefits of being a commissioned officer, even an acting one. Added responsibilities clearly took his mind off personal concerns and served to speed time along, alleviating boredom and monotony that had always plagued him so. If he could lose himself in his job, war-fighting might just become easier. Perhaps deep involvement was what enabled an Eisenhower, Bradley or Patton to handle pressure for long periods of time. If this were so, Bauer need not be so concerned about going under when next he went into battle. However, a disturbing reminder challenged his theory.

Perhaps it was the re-visitation of times past at Fort Riley, but Don Bauer succumbed one tormenting night. The incubus approached in bits and pieces to coalesce into an apparition from a half-decade ago.

In a restless haze, Don was again climbing Mount Pantano in Italy. He labored with others under heavy load up a steep path on a cold, damp night. They were to seize the four knobs of Pantano, an outpost on the German Winter Line near Cassino. As they moved over the crest, a smattering of small arms fire was joined by the "womp, womp" of mortar rounds exploding.

Don led his understrength squad straight ahead to the first knob sloping downward. There he positioned his six men, told them to shed packs and dig in. Don chopped into the hard, rocky soil to hollow out a place for himself, piling spoil to the front and sides. Not a moment too soon!

German soldiers converged from other knobs in an attack to sweep Americans from their toehold. Don shot at shadows coming out of the darkness below, inciting others to do likewise. Shadows tossed back concussion grenades that exploded all around. Abruptly, friendly incoming artillery screeched overhead to land among attacking Germans. The explosions walked backwards to the very edge of Don's position, sending fragments whizzing overhead. The exposed Germans withdrew then, leaving behind their dead and wounded.

Don got up from the dirt and debris to check his men. All had survived; all were now digging deeper. Everyone knew the enemy would return again and again! Don saw no sign of his platoon leader, Lieutenant Brady, who was somewhere to the rear. During the lull, Don improved on his own hole in the ground.

Daylight broke slowly over the cloud-enshrouded mountain. There would be no sunshine, so they would be chilled all day. Don opened a can of hash and ate the cold chunks, chasing them down with an occasional swig of water from his canteen. He craved hot coffee, but there could be no fires here. Maybe hot chow tonight, though.

Lieutenant Brady crawled up and announced they would attack in an hour or so. Then he crawled on to the next squad, and the next. This was Brady's first battle and he was taking it seriously and cautiously. At about noon they attacked toward the second knob, following friendly artillery fires up the hillside to the very top. Before they could dig in, however, the Germans struck from two sides in a move to pinch off the Americans. Don's squad scrambled back to Knob 1 as friendly artillery pummeled the Germans reoccupying Knob 2 in late afternoon.

No hot chow that evening! Carrying parties had all they could do to replenish ammunition and evacuate the wounded. (The dead were left in place for the time being.) When rain began to fall, Don's men caught water in a shelter half to refill canteens. They attacked toward Knob 2 again but couldn't quite reach the top this time. Again they pulled back under cover of friendly artillery. And so it went for three rain-soaked days and nights.

Benumbed throughout, Don Bauer periodically heard unheeded cries for Medic! and whimpers of the dying. He didn't respond to Lieutenant Brady's plea when he was hit close to Bauer's skimpy shelter. Don's feet were so swollen he could barely walk. What could he do?

Relief came on the fourth day. Bauer and the two remaining men in his squad crawled down the mountain path, sliding frequently on their buttocks because their feet were like water-filled bags. All survivors in Bauer's company were carried away in a single deuce and a half truck, a mere fifth of those who had gone up Pantano the first day. Bauer didn't know if the battle had been won or lost, nor did he care.

"Hey! You're moanin' to beat hell!" the cadet sleeping next to Don in the Fort Riley barracks called out.

"Yeah! You're keeping everyone awake," another shouted.

Embarrassed, Bauer forced himself to stay awake lest he slip back into the nightmare. However, reflections that ensued were no relief. He relived the days following Pantano when grizzled retreads from hospitals, stockades, and rear area units arrived as fillers, an unhappy lot indeed. Lieutenant Morris Martin replaced the late Lieutenant Brady as platoon leader. Don was not impressed initially by the balding, roly-poly replacement officer commissioned via ROTC in the late 1930s.

Lieutenant Martin made Bauer platoon sergeant on recommendation of the company commander. But Don's heart wasn't in it, so he went to Lieutenant Martin's tent one evening for a talk.

"Who's there?" Martin asked when Don announced his presence.

"Sergeant Bauer."

Lieutenant Martin fumbled with ties on the tent opening and admitted Don. Apparently Martin had been in bed, for he stood in his long johns to light the Coleman lantern hanging from a tent pole.

Don sat on a folding chair and observed Lieutenant Martin moving about the tent. A more unlikely leader of men was difficult to imagine, yet this was his platoon leader! Well, Bauer would get right to the point.

"Lieutenant, I won't be your platoon sergeant," Don announced. "I'm burned out. I've had it!"

The pudgy lieutenant was not startled in the least. He nodded his head as if he had expected such reaction. Then he reached inside a musette bag under the cot and extracted a bottle of whisky. He produced two cups and poured a couple ounces of whisky into each. Martin handed one to Don and held up the other in toast-like gesture. After touching cups, both put the containers to their lips and sipped.

"Sergeant Bauer," the lieutenant began. "I believe I understand you. Frankly, I don't want to be a platoon leader. I'm not even sure I'm up to the job. So, what are we going to do?"

Don stared back unblinkingly, thinking the comparison was hardly fair since Martin had just arrived. But Martin wasn't through talking.

"You've had a rough go and deserve a break," the lieutenant continued, "but I can't do anything about that. You've survived and now we need your savvy. There's no one else. So we're both caught up in circumstances we can't do a damned thing about!"

They sipped at the same time, seeking diversion perhaps.

"Sergeant, I'm depending on you," Martin went on. "Let's talk man to man now – no bullshit! I want you to stick around and tell me when I do something stupid. Can you do that?"

Sergeant Don Bauer nodded, begrudgingly impressed by Lieutenant Martin's honesty. Bauer stood up to go, feeling better in two ways: The whisky warmed his gut and Lieutenant Martin just might not be a complete flop after all.

In the time remaining, Lieutenant Martin and Sergeant Bauer prepared their platoon to cross the Rapido River south of Cassino. (This was the time Don and Chuck ducked out to visit the Crotone's with Lieutenant Martin's tacit approval.) In fact, their charges were a little cocky as they moved toward the Rapido River that fateful night.

Lieutenant Martin crossed in the first boat. And he stood upright in the midst of enemy small arms and artillery fire to guide others ashore. On the far side of the Rapido, he led his men to the high ground that was their first objective. He advanced firing his carbine somewhat erratically and tossing grenades awkwardly, as if he had never done those things before. He demanded support-

ing fires from the company commander when his troops were being pounded by enemy mortars. He even helped drag the wounded to comparative safety during a lull in the fighting. He fought furiously during the final crushing German assault until bullets from a machine pistol killed him on the spot. The Germans stopped shooting then; the battle was over.

In dim light, a few remaining GIs scrambled back to the Rapido. Bauer tried to collect them, but they were mindlessly jumping into the river to escape. So Don edged his way into the cold, churning waters and drifted away. Only a trace of Lieutenant Morris Martin's brief fighting legacy survived! Now, five years later, Don Bauer summed it up in a few words: "He was a good one."

Over the course of the summer, Jan and Don had corresponded regularly. He frequently called on weekends and was cheered that she seemed to be handling the separation well. She even suggested they forgo the meeting in Kansas City because her folks might not understand. She would make it all up to him when they were reunited. Under the circumstances, Don agreed.

When summer camp closed, Don returned to Homesite. Brad was still pitching for independent baseball teams that could come up with the hundred dollars per game he charged. Don attended a game and was impressed with his brother's poise and confidence on the mound. Obviously, he had picked up a lot during his time in the minor leagues.

Brad and Dad had bought a car together, but the vehicle was mostly Brad's. He would stay through the fall harvesting and probably come to Iowa City for the second semester if Dad came up with another farming arrangement.

Don called Jan and set up a date two days hence. They would meet in Iowa City as she moved back into her aunt's house for fall semester. So Don was lighthearted when he departed Homesite to meet Jan. However, his mood was soon dampened by a radio news bulletin that foreshadowed an unpredictable future.

Soviet Premier Joseph Stalin was closing Allied rail, water and highway access routes to Berlin in order to force Western Powers out of the pre-war German capital. President Harry Truman warned the Soviets that the United States would not back off, and he promised Berliners an airlift that would keep them supplied with the necessities of life. Don shuddered at the possibilities of this confrontation: Any misstep could lead to open warfare. The question seemed to be not *if* war would come but *when*! Would there be time to finish his last year at Iowa University?

CHAPTER IX

TREKKING THE MAZE

The Berlin crisis was but one surprise in the fall of 1948. Don Bauer took up with Jan Dallas where he had left off in June. The first two days they moved her things back into Aunt Becky's house. They took time to catch up on intimate and social activities, of course. Apparently, their relationship had survived the separation without a hitch.

When they went to Legion Club again, everything seemed the same. They danced sensually and drew attention. Don was immensely proud and thanked his lucky star for having won her over. But a casual remark caused him to wonder.

"Hey! You've changed partners," someone said as Jan walked past.

Don dismissed the remark since Jan retained her poise and acted as though it had not been meant for her. However, another chance comment seemed to upset her. And when she suggested they leave Don became suspicious.

"You never miss a beat," a woman at a nearby table had said in passing. "You'll win every time!"

"Win what?" Don asked on the way to the car.

"It was nothing," Jan said. "She was probably referring to the Open House last spring."

The explanation was plausible and should have sufficed, but Don was obsessed at that point.

"It adds up," he told himself. "The separation, her calling off the trip to Kansas City, plus gratuitous remarks from two strangers. Two and two equals four!"

"Who were you with?" Don asked as they pulled to a stop at her house. Again she said it was nothing, but he wouldn't be put off.

"Jan, you danced with someone at Legion Club this summer," he insisted. "Now, who was it?"

"I went there with Rob."

"How could you?"

"He came by one day for a visit. Later, he asked me out and I went, but it was strictly platonic. He's a friend, that's all."

She studied his countenance, trying to fathom his credulousness. Don stared straight ahead, his jaw firmly set. He was mad! Jan moved next to him, took his hand, asked him to look at her. He did so reluctantly, remaining taut.

"Don, I love you," she vowed. "There will never be anyone else."

"Do you tell him that, too?"

"Don't be that way!"

"He said you always come back to him. I'd say he's right!"

"What if I told you he's quitting school? He's having a bad time. He worries about his health, and he doesn't know what to do with his life."

"So?"

"He needs someone to talk to. As you know, we go back a long way. I can't turn him down now."

"And when he asks to make love?"

"Don't be ridiculous!"

"The two of you danced sensationally, or whatever! I guess he needs that, too."

"We went to Legion Club to talk and then he asked me to dance. How could I say no?"

"Does he dance well?"

"Not as well as you."

"But you won. You won what?"

"The manager sponsored a contest one evening and we were awarded a bottle of champagne."

"So, you danced more than once?"

Jan remained silent.

He now knew she couldn't handle separations. Couldn't be trusted! She would always have opportunities; she would always be tempted. On the other hand, he was not willing to give her up, break it off! Not yet, anyway.

"What do we do now?" he asked in softened voice.

"We go on as before. Nothing has changed."

"Can you hold Rob off?"

"Of course."

"Jan, I'll never share you. I'd leave first."

She snuggled closer, until the warmth of her hip and roundness of her breast distracted him. He drew her closer still and kissed her face and lips.

"We need to go inside," she murmured. And so they did.

A surprise in the Quad, too. Don got his old room back, but not his old roommate. Ed Banyon had dropped out over the summer. Always a quiet individual, Ed had grown increasingly reclusive by July. At Student Health he was diagnosed as a schizophrene. The psychiatrist locked him up, gave him shock treatments, chemicals, and counseling, but Ed had improved very little. When Don visited Banyon in isolation, he broke into a prolonged sobbing spell. Clearly, Ed Banyon wasn't ready for visitors yet, so Don excused himself shortly.

Bauer's new roommate was Les Hallton, just out of high school. Les was outgoing but a serious engineer student. He told Don right away that he admired veterans and was pleased to have a mature roommate to keep him close to the books. Don was satisfied to be back in his old room, felt comfortable with Hallton, and reclaimed his dishwashing job in Quad Cafeteria.

Bob Gotti had news for Bauer as well. Gotti had suffered a heart attack back in July and would not be able to manage Bauer for a while. Gotti hoped to recover fully, which should coincide with his son's discharge from the army early next year.

"Keep in shape, Don, and we'll put it all together next year," Bob Gotti promised.

At registration, Bauer signed up for Spanish, Physiology, Kinesiology, Teaching Methods, Swimming and ROTC. He could handle these subjects, continue outside activities, and pick up remaining degree requirements in spring semester. Don Bauer was comfortably on track.

Upon returning to his room one day, Don found a scroll leaning against the door. He unrolled the 24-by-30-inch parchment to find Rob Stone's painting, which, ironically, had been entitled <u>The Winner</u>. No note accompanied the work, however. As he surveyed Stone's handiwork, Bauer felt guilty as the devil. He waited a while before mentioning the painting to Jan. Then, one day he pulled it from behind the car seat where they were sitting, fully expecting to surprise her. Stoically, she looked at him and said, "I saw it last summer."

"I have a hard time understanding Rob," Don ventured.

"What perplexes you?"

"He should hate me!"

"Maybe he understands."

"Understands what?"

"Understands I love you, but he'll settle for what I can give."

"How pathetic!"

"You're overlooking something, Don," she reminded him. "Rob's not healthy, which handicaps him with women. He's comfortable with me because I accept his condition."

"You could also say he's playing on your pity."

"That's not fair," she rejoined. "Rob and I have shared a lot over the years. We were engaged before you came along, remember?"

"So?"

"Maybe he wants you to understand as well."

Don shook his head in disbelief. What a convoluted arrangement! He was trying to be reasonable but wasn't sure what he could go along with.

"What do you expect me to do?" he asked.

"I'm not sure," she replied thoughtfully. "I'm torn between desire and obligation. I feel I must help Rob, but I want to love you."

"I'm not following you."

"Whatever Rob had in mind ended up terribly ironic. When he showed me the painting last summer, I was benumbed. All my feelings for you welled up, feelings I'd suppressed since you left for Fort Riley. I couldn't bring myself to comment, even though he wanted me to in the worst way."

"Rob watched me for the longest time," she continued. "When I didn't speak, he simply rolled up your picture and put it away. He knew then for sure."

"Knew what?"

"That I love you irretrievably."

"So why doesn't he give up?"

"He's not convinced we – you and I – belong together."

"And why not?"

"He thinks you're using me."

"How so?"

"To solve your problems."

"I have problems?"

"He says you thrash around not knowing what you want. In the meantime, I'm convenient."

"And you, Jan Dallas, what do you think?"

"We seem to get along beautifully, but you won't talk about what happens eventually."

"Who knows the future?"

"Some people have an idea. Rob wants to marry me no matter what. His prospects are dim, but he wants me to be a part of whatever's out there for him. So what about you?"

"Jan, you are my future!"

"You'll marry me?"

"I want to marry you, yes."

"But I need commitment!"

"I'll do whatever it takes to keep you."

"Details, please!"

"We'll marry after graduation, when I have a job."

"Why wait? Others take a chance. Why can't we?"

"I could never marry and not provide for you."

"But we can pool our resources."

"Jan, I have no resources," he said emphatically. "I wish that I did, but you see everything right here. An old car, a GI Bill, and a part-time job. That's it!"

"Our parents could help."

"Not mine. I'd never ask them for anything."

"You're bitter," she said.

"Not any more."

She relaxed against him in the car seat, having unburdened herself. If his response wasn't all that she had hoped for, at least he had been sincere and practical. Truthfully, she would have been reluctant to ask her parents for help, but she had to test him, didn't she?

He was now holding her, stroking her hair, expressing his need for her, which, after all, was the most reassuring thing he could do.

"You're right, Don," she said. "We'll wait. But I don't want anything to happen to what we've put together. And I want no more separations; this summer was terrible!"

"I know," he replied. "And I am trying to go along with Rob, but you must never give in to him."

"You mean sexually?"

"Exactly!"

"I won't," she said.

And so they went on day by day, even as another crisis grew. Stalin made good on his threat to block Allied access to Berlin, and Truman made good on his promise to supply Berliners. The American airlift got underway as planes shuttled back and forth at two-minute intervals round the clock. This contest of wills continued day by day. Still, life went on, defining its whims in unpredictable ways.

In a rush to get to his dishwashing job one evening, Don Bauer ran a red light. He found himself pulled over by a vigilant policeman in the center of town and was issued a summons to appear in court. Subsequently Don was fined $25 and costs, which should have been the entire penalty.

Student journalists routinely perused the police blotter for the <u>Daily Iowan,</u> however. Don's infraction was picked up and appeared under the heading "Student Fined." Now embarrassment had been added – and a need for further accounting!

A note summoned Bauer to Colonel Jackson's office at Don's convenience. Bauer went that very afternoon, not sure what the bidding was about. He got an inkling when he heard Colonel Jackson's glum reception.

"Mr. Bauer," the Colonel said sternly, "I noted you've had a driving violation."

"Sir, I wasn't paying attention," Don explained.

"I'm disappointed," the Colonel continued. "Your evaluations from summer camp were excellent. I've considered you a promising leader."

"It won't happen again, sir."

"End of case," Colonel Jackson announced after a pause. "Next topic. Tell me about your experiences during the war, Mr. Bauer."

Don gave a thumbnail sketch of his time in North Africa and Italy. He understated trauma and his personal role because Colonel Jackson also had been in combat and understood dangers and wartime demands. The Colonel displayed intense interest in everything Don said.

"Would you give a forty-five-minute summation of the Anzio battle?" Colonel Jackson asked when Bauer had finished. "I want veterans to impart their experiences to fellow cadets, and I want you to lead out."

"I'd be glad to try," Don replied.

"Fine, Mr. Bauer," the Colonel said as he stood up. "You'll be scheduled early next semester, but you'll want to start collecting your thoughts right away. Also, put in a request to my Exec for training materials."

Don was flattered by Colonel Jackson's attention; however, he wondered what it might mean for the future. Did the Colonel have something in mind other than a Reserve Officer commission? A tiny seed had been planted in fertile culture; Don Bauer considered Colonel Jackson a "good one."

At times Don missed the excitement of boxing. Without Bob Gotti's prompting, Bauer was becoming sluggish. He still ran two miles a day and punched the light and heavy bags three times a week, but his edge was slipping away. The flip side was that Don and Jan had more time together. She was pleased that he still tried to improve his dancing, even though he was inclined to believe he had peaked.

When Don mentioned that Colonel Jackson had selected him to be the first briefer in a novel ROTC program, Jan accepted the assignment as routine rather than an honor. She went with him to research his briefing, still not realizing this was "something special." Don sorted through military references to get the whole story, but the thread throughout would be his own observations. He requested maps and sketches from the ROTC Department. When he had a workable draft, Don submitted the whole to Colonel Jackson.

The Colonel suggested a few changes and then invited Bauer to rehearse before members of the faculty. Don worked out details with the Exec and at the appointed time appeared for the rehearsal. The faculty members were Colonel Jackson and Major Boardman, who would take over once the program got underway.

Don didn't go in cold. He had practiced on his own several times and had committed the narrative to memory. He used the pointer deftly, and he pointed out locations on sketches and maps. He discussed various personalities, since they were critical to the outcome of the battle. In asides, he told where he himself had been at various stages. "Do as well next week and we're off to a good start," Colonel Jackson said at the finish.

Don hastened to pass the results on to Jan. She made note of his barely concealed elation and asked, "Are you thinking of going back into the Army?"

"I may not have a choice," he responded. "Things with the Soviets don't look so good."

"Others seem less excited," she offered. "Sometimes I think you make more of that than you should."

"No one got excited a decade ago either, but I knew we would go to war."

"Polaris again, isn't it?"

"Maybe."

He settled down then, realizing there was more to this discussion than his performance before the faculty. "Military" meant "separation" to Jan and she wanted none of that! Don took another tack.

"I guess I tend to overblow any little distinction I get academically," he said. "It's probably because my record is spotty, so you have to forgive me."

"Well, you should feel good about being singled out," she ventured, "but I sometimes wonder where this ROTC is leading."

"Who knows?"

She turned demure, but her message was clear: "Just don't jeopardize our relationship!"

"Just wish me well," he said with a smile.

Despite his preparation, Don Bauer was nervous on presentation day. Not doing well before his peers could have embarrassing consequences, of course. Even as he waited in uniform bedecked with ribbons and awards he felt the scrutiny of assembled cadets. Indeed, sweating this out was not unlike the ordeal before a boxing match.

Colonel Jackson, who first explained what the program was to achieve, introduced Don. "Sort of like the referee's instructions," Bauer mused to himself. When the "bell" rang, he moved a bit too quickly going to the lectern. He paused to gather himself, evening up the pages of his narrative, and then began:

> In 1943, hard-pressed Soviets pleaded with Western Allies to open a second front to divert Hitler. But the Dieppe Raid on the coast of France convinced Churchill and Roosevelt that the West was not yet ready. So they scraped together a meager force in the Mediterranean and eventually invaded Italy. It's important to note that planners in Britain never took their eyes off the French coast – unless events forced them to look southward. This, of course, is where Anzio came in. Operation Shingle, it was called.

Don Bauer felt inner excitement as he relived events. He described frustrations that led Allied commanders to try an end run around the enemy's Winter Line with an amphibious landing on the Anzio-Nettuno beaches. Then he sketched out ensuing battles and frustrations on the beachhead itself. He was encouraged by rapt attention accorded by cadets and faculty.

Bauer concluded with lessons learned. First, resources must be sufficient to the undertaking. Second, leaders must be resolute. Third, leaders must prepare to cope with caprice for even good plans go awry.

Fourth, attacks must be executed vigorously to ensure momentum. Finally, irresolution exacts a horrendous cost – some 30,000 Allied soldiers were killed, wounded, captured and medically evacuated during the four months of Operation Shingle.

Afterwards, Colonel Jackson offered his observations, which softened Bauer's criticisms somewhat. "We must never forget that it's lonesome at the top," the Colonel reminded the class. "Nonetheless, Mr. Bauer has set a high standard for the rest of you. We're off to a good start!" The class applauded and several cadets approached afterwards to compliment Don.

Jan was impressed when he told her that he had done well. However, she didn't know quite what to make of his beaming pride. Things military obviously fascinated him beyond the norm for veterans, who were more likely to be cynical at this stage. She wondered about his fascination and what it might portend.

Early the next morning Don's thrashing about and moaning interrupted Les Hallton's sleep. "You're having a bad dream or something," he said when Don finally responded to Hallton's hands-on shaking at three forty-seven a.m. Sweating and anxious, Bauer eventually reoriented himself within the dormitory room.

"Sorry, Les," he mumbled. "That's what you get for having a 'loco' veteran for a roommate."

"Sure you're all right?"

"Yeah, I'm O.K. Go back to sleep."

But things were not that simple. He puzzled over this second flashback in six months after a two-year hiatus. Could this nightmare have been unleashed by Don's resurrecting World War II? Most unsettling was his shattered belief that he had "whipped it" that first year back. Did this portend no escape from trauma that had pulverized his most impressionable years?

Gaps in his ROTC briefing now were insistently filled as Bauer tried to sleep. Specter after specter paraded through the remaining night, marching to the staccato rhythm of machine guns and the drumbeat of artillery. He was heading for shore at Anzio, with enemy shells and bombs sending geysers skyward on all sides.

No letup upon landing, either. Artillery boomed away as the new arrivals double-timed away from the beaches. All around, Don Bauer heard sounds of scraping and digging. Troops weren't just enhancing chances for physical survival; they were digging to soothe frayed nerves as well. Anzio was the most dense and exposed battlefield imaginable. Hardly a square foot of surface was spared the presence of man or accouterment. Generators poured forth a foul smoke day and night to obscure the Allied buildup.

A nervous guide met them a couple miles inland and led Don's squad to prepared defenses south of Cisterna, the pivotal German stronghold. Foxholes and bunkers clustered irregularly across a hillside and within depressions that afforded open fields toward the enemy. To hold himself together, Bauer focused on his men. Since he was the only veteran of the squad, others looked to Bauer for example – how does one behave in such a hellhole? Somehow Don convinced himself that inevitability would not catch up with him here – his "time" would not come at Anzio!

On the third night, Sergeant Bauer led his men out of foxholes and into no-man's land to probe for a gap in enemy lines. However, Don suspected the commander's intent was to shake his men out of a passive mindset. Soon they would attack all out, surely.

Sergeant Bauer followed a precise route to an exact spot. His squad would be sealed off by a wall of artillery fire on both sides. Step out of this protected lane and a GI would be blasted away as quickly as an enemy. Then, too, Don knew an artillery projectile could stray as well as a man could, but an occasional erratic shell was the price of protection.

Sergeant Bauer led up front, following markers warily and cautiously. He had progressed a bare fifty yards when Germans opened up with final protective fires, interlocking streams of bullets that theoretically covered every entry into a defensive position. To be sure, the Alban Heights were a hornets' nest!

Having stirred up the Germans, Bauer followed instructions and withdrew. Sure enough, covering friendly artillery sent rock and debris sailing overhead as GIs gingerly worked their way back. Several suffered minor scratches and bruises, but no one was seriously injured. Sergeant Bauer's neophytes had survived their first engagement.

A thousand artillery pieces shelled known and suspected German fortifications for over an hour when the breakout began two days later. The attack was a blur to Sergeant Bauer. Never had he seen such concentration of sound, force, and fury. The Germans were stunned as well, and Americans quickly secured their objectives. Smoke drifted upward from hundreds of craters in the eerie silence that followed.

So the battle of the Anzio beachhead ended abruptly for Sergeant Don Bauer, but its impact lingered on. A half-decade later in a college dormitory, he again smelled oily smoke, shrunk back from eerie sounds, dodged anti-personnel bomblets, and guarded against lulls. (Lulls were dreaded because they enticed GIs to relax, setting up a deadly scenario for that first enemy shell to sneak in from out of nowhere. Gotcha!)

Don Bauer lay quietly as Hallton dressed for his eight o'clock class. When Les had softly closed the door behind him, Don got out of bed. He had to lose himself again in tasks, classes, and his love affair if he was to escape these recurring phenomena.

CHAPTER X

SIREN'S WOOING

The year 1949 was pivotal for nations and individuals alike. Four years had passed since World War II ended, but peace was elusive. Conflicts raged from the Middle East – Israel consolidating its newly won statehood – to the Far East – Mao Tse-tung's Communists overthrowing Chiang Kai-shek's Kuomintang. Colonies in Asia and Africa struggled variously for independence against France, the Netherlands, Belgium, Portugal, and Great Britain. The Cold War, a titanic contest between East and West that caught up just about everyone, threatened Armageddon via nuclear weapons.

When Chiang fled to Formosa from mainland China, giving up the world's most populous nation, the outlook for democracy dimmed. Pessimists predicted the West would no longer prevail; optimists predicted the West would win out, but not anytime soon. As always, many focused on daily routines, ostrich-like. Some gave up, feeling they could little influence events. And if the Cold War turned hot no one would survive anyway! As always, stalwarts believed something could be done about the present and the future. They believed rationality would prevail and civilization would muddle through. Nonetheless, they had to be realistic about stakes and demands.

Perhaps nuclear war could be avoided if only because it was so dreadful. However, Stalin the dictator was striving to bring all of Europe and all of Asia into the Soviet orbit. The age-old dream of ruling the world was now attainable through technological developments and Marxist ideology. The only barrier was individualism – human beings! If individuals, indeed, could be harnessed as automatons – as communists sought – the Cold War was lost. But if individuals were allowed to think for themselves, democracy would win out.

Thus, the stronghold of individualism – United States of America – became a foil to the Soviets. As the Berlin crisis continued, the United States invited eleven European nations to Washington and formed the North Atlantic Treaty Organization (NATO). The United States also stepped up nuclear-weapons production and improved delivery systems. It also increased its armed forces, albeit slowly. More junior military leaders were now needed to man divisions and training centers. ROTC was added as a source of Regular Army officers, a move Colonel William Jackson at Iowa University was aware of.

Senior ROTC students were told of the new program during classes. Don Bauer was receptive because he believed he would be called back if war came. He would have no choice! However, he kept such thoughts to himself for the most part.

In the meantime, he heard from Bob Gotti. Gotti had recovered fully and lined up a fight for Don in Cedar Rapids in three weeks. Bauer would fight the three, three-minute-round, main event against Ken Shoemaker, an inexperienced, young, light heavyweight, and would be paid $60 for training expenses. Don decided to discuss this offer with Jan before agreeing.

She was disappointed. Jan had hoped that part of his life was over. She thought he should be looking into things that would enhance post-graduation employment. There was yet another consideration.

"What if you are hurt?" she asked. "Surely, a sixty-dollar purse is not worth that."

"I'll be ready," he promised. "I'll not get hurt!"

She went along eventually, especially when he said this would be his last match. But her sentiment revealed itself when she chose not to attend the fight. "Get it over quickly," she pleaded.

The buildup surpassed that of any previous Bauer fight. Posters of him and Shoemaker appeared prominently throughout the region, including Iowa City. Newspaper and radio sports news hyped the fight as well. The promoter was going all out!

Gotti, displaying renewed enthusiasm, scouted Shoemaker and prepared Bauer mentally while getting him ready physically. Don weighed 170 pounds going in, well under the light heavyweight limit, but Gotti wanted him lighter still. "At 165 you'll be fast and strong," Gotti enthused.

"What about Shoemaker?" Don asked.

"He'll come in at 178, 179 after eating, but that's not good weight. He'll be too slow for you."

To ready himself for three-minute rounds, Don Bauer increased roadwork to five miles a day, worked out on both light and heavy punching bags, shadow boxed, and sparred with other fighters in Gotti's stable. He reduced sugar and starches in his diet and a week before the fight weighed 168 pounds, right on target. Over the next few days, the remaining three pounds would melt away through exercise and dehydration.

Don's only concern was in not having a suitable sparring mate. As it was, he trained with a lightweight and a welterweight, which increased his own speed afoot but not his punching power. Alas, he was not training to handle a big man physically. But Gotti was not concerned: "If you were inexperienced, I'd feel different. But you've always handled big guys easy."

Since Jan didn't go, Don rode with Gotti and the others. He was uncharacteristically relaxed, which he attributed to confidence. After all, he had been on this circuit four years now. Surely, he was a journeyman who had seen it all.

He was further encouraged when he met Shoemaker. The youth appeared so intimidated he couldn't look Bauer in the eye. Shoemaker also appeared a bit flabby and stood two inches shorter than Bauer. Perhaps Gotti was right about this fight.

In the dressing room, Don went through his pre-fight drill perfunctorily. He wondered why he had always been so uptight before. Ironically, he had finally learned to deal with the pressure just as he was phasing out of boxing. As he waited at the edge of the crowd during the last preliminary, Don had a twinge of doubt. Perhaps it was the boisterous crowd that unnerved him momentarily; however, it passed as he entered the ring and received a warm reception. Some of his best fights had been here in Cedar Rapids and the fans remembered.

Al Nemow's instructions bored Don, but Shoemaker listened intently. This was his first big fight and he wanted to get it right. Actually, Nemow seemed unduly interested in refereeing a crowd-pleaser. "Let's give them their money's worth!" he exhorted at the finish.

Back in Don's corner, Gotti vigorously massaged Bauer's neck. Then Gotti inserted the mouthpiece and advised: "Box him the first two minutes. Then pop him good."

When they squared off at center ring, Don speared Shoemaker with two quick left jabs. Both landed, snapping the shorter man's head back. The crowd cheered at the quick start. When Shoemaker drew back, his corner man shouted, "Go after him, Ken. Go after him!" Don braced himself for the lunge sure to come, sticking his left repeatedly in Shoemaker's face and circling right.

Ken Shoemaker shook off left jabs and put everything he had into one punch, a straight right to Don's head. It landed! Squarely! Had Bauer been moving in, he would have been knocked out, surely. Instead, he staggered back, clearly stunned. Instinctively, he tied up the now excited Shoemaker.

"How bad?" Don wondered.

Nemow pushed them apart without a second thought. "Mix it! Mix it!" he urged and waved them to fight on.

"Get him! Get him!" Shoemaker's corner man shouted. "He's hurt!"

The stocky fighter moved in swinging. Don Bauer jabbed back and circled away from the wild right hand. From out of the din, Bauer picked up Gotti's clarion call: "Nail him, Don! Nail him!"

"A minute to go," Bauer told himself. "I'll make it!"

Bauer was not aware of having been hit solidly again; he was about out of the woods now. His head was clearing and he was evading Shoemaker's bull-like rushes. Then he nailed Shoemaker with a clean left hook just before the bell. Although it barely fazed the aggressive young boxer, the punch evoked cheers from the crowd. Don Bauer was still in the fight!

During the break, Gotti held smelling salts under Don's nose, searched his eyes, and asked Bauer to count fingers. Don was more concerned with the numbness in his face. Also, blood trickled from his nose and his eyes were swelling shut. As the minute's rest wound down, Gotti said, "Get on your bicycle, Don. He's coming at you!"

And Shoemaker did! When he wasn't swinging wildly, he was using his bulk and weight to wrestle Bauer about the ring. Anticipating a knockout, the crowd was on its feet. Still somewhat dazed, Bauer managed to avoid blows, cover up in clinches, and fend off the wild man before him. Shoemaker won the second round by a clear margin.

Injured and outclassed at that stage, Bauer himself believed the fight would be stopped between rounds. Indeed, Nemow came to his corner and pretended to look over Don's injuries as a prelude to calling the fight. His intentions were otherwise, however.

"Come on, Don," Nemow chided. "Make a fight of it! The crowd's getting restless."

At the bell, Gotti placed the mouthpiece behind Don's swollen lips and shoved his charge toward ring center. Don Bauer was on his own in this fight. Still, he was glad Jan Dallas was not there; she would have had him quit!

Bauer made a fight of it. He smashed a straight right to Shoemaker's jaw, staggering him to the crowd's delight. Shoemaker charged in again and took a left hook to the side of the head. He jumped back and gathered himself for yet another try. But Bauer moved in, poking jab after jab into the bobbing face before him. The crowd cheered Don on, calling for a knockout. For a while, Bauer thought he might just pull it off.

But youth was served that evening. Shoemaker collected himself, used his bulk to wear Bauer down, and finished with a rush to win the split decision. In essence, Shoemaker had won with that first big punch!

"Your nose is mangled," Gotti said in the dressing room as Don applied an ice pack. He felt no pain – had no feeling at all in his face. His eyes were slits, and he could breathe only through his mouth. Al Nemow was contrite when he dropped by.

"Maybe I shoulda stopped it, Don," he said. "But you and I both know the crowd wouldn't a liked it." What Nemow said was absolutely right, of course. But Don Bauer took consolation at another level: Jan Dallas would be pleased that his boxing career was assuredly over.

When they stopped for something to eat on the way back to Iowa City, Don could only sip liquids. Further, he was embarrassed by the swelling and bleeding, so he insisted they not tarry long. When Gotti dropped him off at the Quad, Don promised to go to Student Health, but didn't say when.

He called Jan. When he told her that he had lost, she said, "I heard it on the radio. Are you hurt badly?"

"I'll be O.K."

"Do you want to come over?" she asked.

"I'd rather not," he replied. "And, Jan, you were right."

She paused before saying, "Sleep in tomorrow and I'll see you at one."

Don had awakened his roommate, of course. "Sorry ol' buddy," Hallton said after surveying Bauer's damaged face. "I'd better take you to Student Health."

"Not tonight, Les. I'm bushed."

Although Bauer had undressed and crawled into bed, Hallton still attempted to get Don to a doctor. When Don wouldn't budge, Hallton soaked a wash cloth in cold water and placed it across Don's nose.

"This'll help," he said, "but an ice bag would be better."

"Thanks, Les. The cloth'll do just fine."

Don slept fitfully. He was up a couple times to re-soak the washcloth, which alleviated dryness in his mouth and throat. When Hallton got up early for his eight o'clock class, he gave Bauer two aspirin tablets and some advice: "Get over to Student Health as soon as you can, ol' buddy."

Bauer stayed in bed, uncertain about his next step. He came to a decision only after Maudie, the maid, opened the door to clean the room and saw him. Maudie wasted no time.

"Get to the doctor or I'll call an ambulance!" she threatened.

"That bad, huh?"

"You're darn right it is! Now get out of that bed and go!"

Nor was he accorded sympathy at Student Health. The female doctor took one look and started to call the police.

"Who assaulted you?" she demanded.

"I lost a boxing match," Don explained.

"When?"

"Last night."

"Why didn't you come then?" she chided. "Those bones have started to knit. Now we'll have to rebreak them."

Bauer found empathy at Eye, Ear, Nose and Throat, however. The doctor had boxed at Michigan State in his student days and appreciated Don's reluctance to admit any serious damage. Workmanlike, the doctor inserted a pry in Don's nostrils one at a time and opened breathing passages. The procedure – especially the eerie sensation of popping bones and cartilage – was squeamish but it was not painful for Don, really.

Next, the doctor packed Bauer's nostrils with medicated gauze and taped a wax splint over his upper face. Notches had been cut out for eyeholes, so Don resembled a man from Mars. The doctor gave Don a bottle of aspirin, told him to return in three days, and sent him on his way.

Don was reluctant to face Jan. People had stared as he went to his car, so how would she react? He drove to Fine Arts building and waited for her class to end. She spotted his car and hurried to get in. She looked him over without speaking. Don knew what she was thinking and appreciated her restraint. The last thing he needed now was to be second-guessed.

"Let's take a ride," he suggested.

"Fine."

They drove north out of Iowa City, not talking. Finally, he said, "I don't blame you for ignoring me. I'm a mess."

"You're certainly a curiosity. But so what!"

He felt better then and his hand drifted to her lap. On the spur of the moment he turned into the parking lot of the Lighthouse, an eatery on the right. Few cars were there, indicating few patrons inside.

"Are you too embarrassed to go in with me?" he asked.

"Don't be silly," she replied and opened the door to get out.

The lunch crowd was sparse, so they were seated with little commotion. After Don ordered two beers and hamburgers, she took his hand in both of hers and asked, "Can you chew?"

"If I can't, I starve," he said in jest.

She patted his hand and smiled winsomely. The gesture overwhelmed him and tears welled in his eyes. God, he loved her! The facial splint disguised his emotional breakup from others there – but not from Jan! She had not seen him cry before and sensed he did not want to be seen doing so now. She pretended not to notice.

The waiter brought beer at that point, so he quickly took a sip and said, "Tastes good."

"Yes it does," she agreed after following suit.

"I should have listened to you, Jan," he continued.

"You had to do what you had to do," she said. "That's Polaris."

The waiter brought the hamburgers, again interrupting them. Don used a knife to cut the sandwich into tiny bits. Gingerly, he put the first morsel into his mouth with a fork and began to chew, slowly. The taste served to revive and cheer him.

Left to her thoughts for the moment, Jan pondered his self-conscious behavior. He was not handling his condition well. Why, he might just hibernate in his room until the splint came off! No doubt about it, she had to snap him out of the mind set.

Only a middle-aged man, a waiter and a bartender remained in the room at the time, so Jan went to the nickelodeon and inserted a coin. She punched the button for <u>Begin the Beguine</u> and returned. As the lilt began, Jan took Don's hand invitingly.

"Not now, Jan," he protested.

She ignored his reluctance, tugged him to his feet and led the way to the small dance floor. They set a Rumba pose and began dancing. It was a curious sight, this dance by a masked man and a pretty woman pretending nothing was out of the ordinary. The moment was not lost on those watching. Afterwards, the other patron, the waiter, and the bartender applauded. Then the waiter brought two more beers, compliments of the house.

"Now you, too, have won a dance contest," Jan kidded.

"But Rob won Champagne!" he rejoined.

Don slipped back into his routine the next day. The only persisting discomfort was a dry mouth, but he kept a wet cloth over his face when he slept and gutted it out. On the third day, the EN&T doctor removed the splint and gauze and apologized for the coloring that remained around Don's eyes and cheekbones.

"Just consider it a badge of honor, my boy," the doctor quipped. "I always did!"

As it turned out, others did, too. Don, as a prospective Regular Army officer, appeared before an evaluation panel that same week. When he explained his appearance, panel members seemed impressed that he was a boxer.

"And a good one," according to Colonel Jackson who was present.

Then for a time, prospects for international peace seemed to improve. The Soviets backed down on Berlin and reopened routes to the beleaguered city. Perhaps Stalin had learned that the West would be steadfast in its resolve. But, then, maybe he was following a two-step-forward, one-step-backward approach. Stalwarts considered the second possibility more likely, especially when the Soviets exploded an atomic device that fall.

Jan and Don attended the Apple Blossom Ball in April. She wore a dazzling green formal gown that drew attention. They were at their dancing best early on; however, the mood changed over the course of the evening. Their college days were running out and they were now faced with post-commencement planning – the inevitability they had been avoiding.

Recently, they had gone to an open house to be interviewed by various high schools seeking teachers. He quickly learned schools were looking for names to coach baseball, basketball, and baseball. Recruiters were not interested in boxers, however, even one with a "name." He was qualified to teach History, English, Government, Biology, and minor sports, but these soft subjects were not in demand either.

Jan, on the other hand, was in demand. She was certified to teach Music, Dance, Sociology, Physics, and Geology, plus she was just two courses short of a Master's Degree. Although highly employable, Jan was inclined to pursue higher education. Much depended on what he did, however.

The economy was slow in the Midwest that year, especially in the non-agricultural sectors. When Don contacted businessmen he had befriended through boxing – those who had invited him to do so over the years – no one had anything to offer at this time. All would keep their eyes open, and they were willing to provide recommendations. However, Don shied from approaching acquaintances and relatives back in Homesite because, indeed, it appeared he had wasted his time in Phys Ed and boxing.

But there was a possibility. Colonel Jackson called him in for a career discussion. The Colonel said Bauer had a very high evaluation score from the Regular Army Panel. Colonel Jackson, too, believed Bauer had a bright future as an officer.

"I can practically guarantee you acceptance under the Distinguished Military Graduate program," he said.

Don agreed to put in his papers and go for a physical examination if the application was accepted at higher headquarters. Then he finally brought up the matter with Jan Dallas, first referring to the disappointments he experienced during job interviews she was aware of. The approach did not work well with her, however.

"Do you know what you're doing?" she asked sternly.

"I've just put you in shock."

"Worse than that! You've told me you're ending our relationship."

"You're carried away," he cautioned. "It's not that harsh."

"After all I've said, you're thinking of joining the Army. What is it with you?" As he fumbled for a reply, she plunged on: "Rob was right! You've been using me. You never had any intention of marrying me – ever!"

"That's not so," he protested. "I'm still trying to work things out."

"Such as?"

"I'll go back home and see what I can uncover there," he said in desperation.

"Any prospects?"

"Nothing specific."

And that's where matters stood during the Apple Blossom Ball the evening that ended on a subdued note. As a matter of fact, they were barely speaking to one another when they reached Aunt Becky's house. Neither felt comfortable as they lay in bed together that night. Even when they arranged themselves as always, a divide remained: Bodies were aligned, minds were adrift.

"Now we know how it ended," she said eventually, pushing the rift.

"How did it end?" he asked, stalling.

"You go into the Army and I stay here. That's what you've wanted all along. This college phase ends and you chase Polaris in a dreamlike trance, blindly, ploddingly without the slightest idea where you end up. Or with whom!"

"Not so."

"What then? pray tell."

"I'm not sure. I'm keeping options open, but I haven't committed to anything."

"What about grad school?"

"My grades aren't good enough."

"But you've said they've been lenient with veterans."

"I don't know. And how would I pay for it?"

"Don't you have some GI Bill left?"

"A few months, but not enough."

"Why not find out? Check into it," she urged.

"O.K.," he said, if only to close out the spat that night.

"I'll finish my Master's in January," she asserted. "Then I'll work full time and help us get started."

"Jan, I love you."

"I love you, too."

They slept soundly on that note. And Don checked things out over the next few days. He had nine months remaining on the GI Bill, which would enable him to start grad school. As for his eligibility, despite recent improvement his grade point was still too low. However, he might be admitted on probation, since he had garnered a B+ average over the past two years. Don requested admission.

Graduation rituals lacked luster because Don and Jan both intended to stay on in Iowa City. He turned down the Distinguished Military Graduate offer for Regular Army, but accepted a Reserve Officer's commission tendered through senior ROTC. He made it a point to thank Colonel Jackson for efforts in Don's behalf.

"I may still see you in uniform," the Colonel said good-naturedly. "There could be a call up, you know."

"If I'm called up, I hope to serve with you, sir," Don replied.

"That possibility might not be so remote," Colonel Jackson opined. "I'm being assigned to the Infantry School at Fort Benning, Georgia, this fall. You could be sent there for a course of some sort."

Despite that possibility, Don Bauer put military service out of his mind. He rummaged about for an area of graduate study and chanced upon an opening. Dr. Harold Beckley was testing and measuring star athletes in a search for predictors of future performance. He had subjects from football, basketball, baseball, track, and wrestling, but none from boxing. When Dr. Beckley learned Don was a boxer, he asked Don to participate. Bauer agreed and stumbled onto something.

After putting Don through speed, strength, and agility tests, Beckley asked Don to assist him in testing other subjects. Don jumped at the opportunity to shore up his chances for grad school, come up with a project of his own, and earn a modest stipend. Maybe Phys Ed and boxing hadn't been a waste of time after all!

Don and Jan talked then of getting married when he finished grad school. Since she hadn't met his family, they went to Homesite over a weekend in October. They stayed with Deborah and Paul, whose farm-house had indoor plumbing. Besides, Paul was now farming the home place in addition to his own farm. Everyone seemed satisfied with this arrangement, especially since none of the Bauer boys wanted to come back home to stay.

Saturday night, they went dancing at the parish hall. Mom and Dad didn't go, of course, and Frank, who did not visit Homesite much anymore, was not there. Jeanne and Verne had set it all up and they kept the party going. Brad and his girlfriend were there from Grand Island, Nebraska, where he had a job selling agricultural products and playing independent baseball. That is where he had met Linda Crowe and they were now dating seriously.

Jan and Don restrained their dancing under the circumstances. Still, they attracted attention with esoteric routines and Jan's attractiveness. She danced with others throughout the evening, and, in Don's estimation, was the hit of the party. Jeanne boasted that she herself had started Don dancing and look at him now! Uncle Walt dropped by and was promptly smitten by Jan. She danced with him once and then discreetly turned him down thereafter.

After Mass on Sunday, where Jan acquitted herself well in the face of curiosity and unfamiliarity all around, they gathered at the Bauer house for Mom's fried chicken and apple pie. The family get-together broke up in early afternoon when Brad and Linda returned to Grand Island.

"Don't be surprised if you're asked to be a best man next year," Brad alerted Don upon departure. "I'll return the favor when you and Jan finally tie the knot."

Don and Jan returned to Iowa City Sunday evening content that things had gone well. Actually, Don was a bit smug. Uncle Walt, the pharmacist, and other Homesite influentials had been convinced they had underestimated Don Bauer. Although he hadn't always been certain in charting a course, his judgements ultimately had been validated. To be sure, in bleak and lonely times there can be no more reliable guide than Polaris! Of this he was certain.

Chapter XI

Ill Winds Blow

Jan Dallas was awarded a Master's Degree in Fine Arts at the end of January 1950 and accepted a part-time teaching position in the university Music Department. Don Bauer had worked off his probationary status and was now fully enrolled in graduate school. He was taking Research Methods, Logic, and Spanish. He hoped to complete advanced-degree requirements in January 1951. Their personal accommodations remained the same; he lived in the Quad and she with Aunt Becky. Thus, on a personal level, the decade started on a promising note.

The international scene had lurched ominously, however. Presumably, the Soviets were building a nuclear stockpile, which not only unsettled western nations but weakened their much-needed diplomatic leverage. The Soviet Union and China continued to probe in all directions as they sought to expand communism's sway. Thus, considerable thrusting and adjusting were underway as the West sought to contain communist countries through international diplomacy backed by armed might.

In late 1949, the United States – following the lead of the Soviets who had departed North Korea a year earlier – withdrew occupation troops from South Korea. (American advisors stayed to assist building up the South's fledgling armed forces, however.) This withdrawal, plus ambiguity on whether the United States would defend South Korea, tempted North Korea's Premier Kim Il Sung to reunite the divided peninsula.

With Stalin's approval, North Korea's Army struck across the 38th Parallel without warning on June 25th, 1950. The North, much stronger and better equipped, overran the South's defenders and seized Seoul, Capital of South Korea. But the communists had miscalculated: The Korean peninsula now was considered too important to the West to be given up without a fight.

President Harry Truman sent American air power to delay the onslaught and set in motion a United Nations' (UN) effort to halt the invasion. The UN followed Truman's lead and condemned the North for unprovoked aggression. In the meantime, Kim II Sung's forces continued southward, seemingly unstoppable.

General Douglas MacArthur assumed command of UN Forces in Korea and sent occupation troops from Japan onto the battlefields. A Marine Division was dispatched from the United States and several Army divisions were alerted to follow. Other UN Members also sent units as Korea grew into a major conflict.

Americans suffered heavily in early fighting, so back in the states reservists and conscriptees were called to fill depleted ranks. Small-unit leaders were needed too, so newly commissioned second lieutenants were added to the call up in mid-August. Lieutenant Don Bauer was one of those called.

Don was to report to Fort Benning, Georgia, within thirty days for a refresher course. Physically, he could uproot and keep this appointment, of course, but emotionally he had complications. An irate Jan Dallas second-guessed Don Bauer this time.

"Couldn't you see this coming?" she asked.

"I foresaw a possibility, but we discussed that when I signed up for ROTC. Remember?"

"But you shouldn't have signed up!" she snapped. "Most veterans shunned ROTC."

"That's academic now," he reminded her. "I'm committed."

"How long will you be in?"

"Two years. Less if the war ends."

"Will you go to Korea?"

"I'd say not, especially since I was in the last war," he hedged.

She paused, looked directly at him, and asked, "What about our plans?"

"If I'm assigned stateside after the refresher course, you can join me. But whatever, you're in my future."

Jan resigned herself to the inevitable then, as did he. He arranged an interruption of his studies so that he could take up where he left off upon returning. He took delivery on a new two-door Ford coupe in late August and felt a pang of nostalgia as he traded in the old car. The new car lost some of its splendor under the circumstances, but they used it for long summer drives. They also went for evening walks, nighttime riverbankings, and weekend dances – even as news from Korea grew ever more grim.

He told Jan goodbye on September 13th and drove straight through to Fort Benning. He kept himself awake by listening to the radio and was somewhat encouraged by news bulletins on Korea. The UN force was holding its own and even counterattacking from time to time. General MacArthur announced that the Pusan Perimeter would hold, and that the North Koreans would be driven back. The prediction was not an idle boast.

The North Koreans had obsessively closed on the perimeter, pouring everything into a drive to push U.N. forces into the sea. Even massive air power had not slowed the attackers perceptibly and their success seemed assured. Paradoxically, enemy myopia had played right into General MacArthur's scheme of things.

On September 15th – the day Don Bauer reported in to Fort Benning – the flamboyant American general sent an amphibious task force into the rugged Inchon landing area. The move caught North Koreans by surprise and succeeded spectacularly. In effect, enemy forces to the south were destroyed and the remnants could only scramble northward to save themselves.

But MacArthur gave the battered enemy no respite. He sent UN forces northward in pursuit and by mid-October the Yalu River and complete victory were in sight. Understandably, there was now talk fighting would end by Thanksgiving and troops would be home by Christmas.

In the meantime, Lieutenant Bauer became engrossed in his refresher course. He met again several former cadets from the Fort Riley summer camp of 1948, all now second lieutenants readying themselves for the real thing this time. However, as news from the battlefields improved, they, too, began to think of an early release. An old acquaintance was to disabuse Lieutenant Bauer in forthright manner.

After three weeks at Fort Benning, Don looked up his erstwhile mentor. He found Colonel Jackson in his office as Director of Weapons Department. The Colonel was pleased to see him – but not surprised.

"You're back where you belong," Colonel Jackson said.

"My fiancee would not agree," Don cautioned.

"Oh, she'll come around," the Colonel reassured him. "They always do."

Don wasn't so sure, but he was distracted by a confidential bit of news. Speaking in lowered voice, Colonel Jackson revealed he would be going to Korea when another regimental commander was needed. He was pleased at the prospects, and told Don he would be a welcome addition to Colonel Jackson's regiment when the time came.

"What if the war ends?" Don asked.

"Oh, that won't make any difference," Colonel Jackson rejoined. "We've got a way to go over there and they'll need lieutenants for quite a while yet."

In other words, "forget it!" Colonel Jackson was right, of course. Infantry was always the first in and the last out. Clearly, there would be no early out for Lieutenant Don Bauer. On that sobering thought, Don bid Colonel Jackson farewell.

For the third time in his lifetime, Don Bauer was qualifying in use of an infantryman's tools. There were some changes – he now fired a carbine instead of an M-1 rifle – and there were new weapons – a recoilless rifle and a 3.5-inch rocket launcher – but there was a sameness throughout. All infantry weapons were essentially an extension of flesh-and-blood men. More lethal, of course, but not all that different from a pair of boxing gloves, really.

Don naturally took to physical fitness. Lieutenants had to be better conditioned than the men they led, not only to set an example but to meet job demands. Throughout history, fatigue has plagued military leaders, clouding their judgments and encouraging short cuts. Then, too, physical activity enables an officer to deal with stress. Given these realities Lieutenant Bauer wholeheartedly engaged in calisthenics, PT tests, speed marches, and mass games.

He found tactics intriguing, if only because there were so many variables to ponder. Axiomatically, the enemy's location, preparations, and capabilities had to be addressed and a scheme prescribed for friendly formations and weapons support. He realized how shallow his own tactical knowledge had been during World War II; he had led from an instinctual rather than an analytical bent. Along this line, Korean veterans already had been added to the Benning faculty, telling those about to go what to expect.

At the end of the eight-week course, Lieutenant Don Bauer was among five out of two hundred to be awarded the Expert Infantryman's Badge. He had more or less expected the award since he had "rehearsed" often enough. Still, he received a note from Colonel Jackson congratulating him on being an achiever. Perhaps the award was more significant than Don had first believed.

On the home front, emphasis was decidedly elsewhere. Whenever she wrote or called, Jan always inquired if he had received orders. She was elated when he was notified that he would be held over thirty days to be a tactical officer for a Noncommissioned Officers' course. Since he wouldn't be going to Korea before year's end at least, who knew what might eventuate. Perhaps a stateside assignment was not farfetched.

Don doubted he was off the Korea hook, however. Just delayed, perhaps. Nonetheless, he did not discourage Jan's optimism and made plans for her to join him in Columbus, Georgia, as soon as possible. Also, he applied for parachute-jump school immediately following the NCO course in mid-December. Perhaps qualification as a paratrooper might influence his permanent assignment. Then, too, during World War II, he had wanted to be a paratrooper but was not given the opportunity. As long as he was in the army again, why not pursue this yearning?

Jan took two weeks to arrange her departure from Iowa City and arrived in Columbus just before Thanksgiving holiday. They rented a furnished apartment for thirty days. When the landlord assumed they were married, they let it go at that.

Jan found her first exposure to the "old south" of more than passing interest. She made acquaintances with a couple students' wives, who also assumed Jan and Don were married. With so much personnel turbulence, they managed to carry off their little deception without a hitch. Then, too, a reversal of fortunes in Korea foreshortened her stay in Georgia.

Some 300,000 Chinese soldiers slipped into the mountains of North Korea that fall and prepared to attack UN forces. A few skirmishes occurred in October, but in late November the Chinese went all out. Aided by harsh winter weather, Chinese soldiers threatened to cut off and destroy MacArthur's widely scattered units. In what amounted to "an attack to the rear," UN Troops managed to extricate themselves and withdraw to defensible positions below the 38th Parallel.

In view of the precarious military situation, General MacArthur threatened to "nuke China back into the stone age." Political repercussions, including threats to impeach President Truman, added to general disillusionment back in the States. At that stage, the Korean Conflict was becoming a disaster of the first order. More units and replacements from the United States were soon on their way to "frozen Chosin," a cruel switch from the home-by-Christmas scenario.

Don's orders for Korea arrived in mid-December, just as he completed the tactical-officer assignment. His reporting date to Fort Lawton, Washington, was February 1st. Jan Dallas and Don Bauer could harbor no more illusions after that. Gone were hopes for an early out. Gone were idyllic times for young lovers.

In the interim, Lieutenant Bauer would take airborne training while still at Benning. He would finish the course in time to take a two-week leave prior to embarking for overseas. So they closed out their first home together just before Christmas and Jan returned to Iowa City.

He put her on a train in downtown Columbus and watched her walk down the coach aisle to a seat on the far side. As the train pulled away, she waved a disheartened goodbye. Even their prospective reunion in Iowa City three weeks hence was not consoling. Her worst fears had been confirmed.

Don kept busy, of course. With just a couple days off for Christmas, he engaged in rigorous jump training. P.T., pushups, mock-up drills, exit jumps, tower jumps, parachute landing falls, and inspections. Happy Hours at day's ending took up remaining time and occupied his mind for the most part. Comradery helped too. All knew they were going to Korea – and combat – which contributed to an ambience that Don found familiar and even reassuring.

Lonely hours at night that happy-hour beers could not smother were the pit's bottom. Questions and doubts could not be avoided all the time. What was Jan up to? How was she coping? Would she wait for him? Her letters and phone calls said all the right things at the right times, but revealed nothing. Deep down he knew she was already bracing herself for the ordeal to begin on February 1st.

Don made his first live jump in the third week of training. The first two weeks had been grueling and repetitious, but the third was fun. Excitement built when the plane took off. When he stood up and hooked up, he was reminded of entering the boxing ring for a match. He was benumbed emotionally, tensely alert physically. He stood third man back in the stick, so he had but a short distance to shuffle forward to the exit door of the C-82 cargo aircraft. He grasped the sides and stared straight out at the horizon as wind whipped his face. The jump master tapped his thigh and he leaped outward, arms folded across his reserve chute, chin tucked down across his chest, and he counted, "Thousand and one, thousand and two,... ."

The jolt of the parachute opening exceeded his expectations but the tranquility of the descent made it all worthwhile. He floated lazily, safely apart from others, for a seemingly long time. He did not look directly down but picked up the ground peripherally. Gauging treetop height, he put his feet together and flexed his knees slightly. He was surprised when his feet touched earth and he rolled to dissipate momentum. He grabbed parachute lines, swung his legs about, dug in his heels, rose to his feet, and chased a still billowing chute. He quickly outran the chute so that it collapsed. Jump number one had been picture perfect!

And so were the next two. But the fourth jump almost proved his undoing as a paratrooper. He was at the head of the stick when the jump master told him to act as wind dummy. The C-82 would pass over the drop zone, Don would be tapped out, and he would not steer during the drift downward so that the officer in charge could adjust the approach for other jumpers. Since the wind was moderate, little danger was involved – even for a novice.

Don's exit went well, but as he neared the ground among trees he looked downward for a clear landing spot and was startled at how fast he was falling. Instinctively, his legs tensed and he went straight in rather than rolling to one side. A sharp pain shot up his back and took his breath away. He had regained his feet and collapsed the chute when the officer in charge drove up in a jeep.

"What were you doing?" the Captain asked sternly.

"Just getting on the ground," Don gasped.

"Looked like you tried to land standing up," the Captain observed. "Did you hurt yourself?"

"I'm all right."

A sergeant approached from the edge of the drop zone, so the officer in charge, who had to get training jumps underway, drove off. The sergeant, carrying a clipboard to record names of those needing more parachute landing fall (PLF) training, asked, "Captain get your name?"

"He got me all right," Don replied evasively.

"That was about the worst PLF I ever saw," the sergeant commented. "I'll see *you* later."

As he slowly rolled up his chute, Don wondered if he were seriously hurt. The pain lingered in the small of his back; however, he could walk all right if he planted his feet carefully. But practicing PLFs, when he would repeatedly drop off a six-foot-high platform onto the ground and go into a roll, was out of the question. That would kill him. Yet he had to get that last qualifying jump in tomorrow – somehow!

Back in the area, Don held his breath when names were called for remedial PLFs. But his name was not called. Apparently, the captain and sergeant had let the ball drop between them and he had escaped. Now he had a chance.

He went back to his quarters and took a hot shower. As best he could, Don applied liniment to his back. He skipped happy hour but went to supper, where the food improved his outlook. Back in his room, he tried stretch exercises very carefully before crawling into bed not encouraged.

During the night, breathing at times was painful. Every turn of his body was hurtful. When he got out of bed the next morning, his legs seemed sluggish and his back stiffened. He took another hot shower and again rubbed on liniment. After breakfast he was quite sure he could gut it out.

Jolts from double-timing to the airfield were not as severe as he had feared. In fact, running warmed him, relaxed him overall. Harnessing up was taxing, but a nearby student helped with the tugging and pulling. He was further encouraged when the harness became a "corset" bracing his back. He mounted steps to the plane slowly, but still managed to conceal his injury from the jump master. He now had it made because everything was down hill from there on. Why, he could literally fall out the door if he had to.

The opening shock was severe, but a relief eventually – a form of traction perhaps. He didn't enjoy this particular descent because of his dread of ultimately hitting the ground. He stared at the horizon, did not anticipate the impact. He kicked to loosen his legs and then brought his feet together, flexed his knees, and went into a roll without pause. Accompanying pain was dull, manageable. Elated, he swung about, planted his feet, and stood up to outrun the chute. He had pulled it off! He was now a qualified paratrooper! Yes, indeed!

The next morning, Lieutenant Bauer went on sick call. The doctor check the X-ray and reported no serious bone or cartilage damage. Probably a severe muscle strain, he concluded, which should heal itself over time.

After graduation parade that afternoon, Don loaded his car and set off for Iowa City and Jan Dallas on a drizzly day. Because of back discomfort, he did not drive straight through this time. Instead, he reached Iowa City late the next day January 14th, 1951.

Chapter XII

Destiny's Way

Lieutenant Don Bauer, ordered to a puzzling war in Korea, took a room in the Jefferson Hotel. He had two weeks' leave, money in his pocket, and was about to meet with the exciting Jan Dallas. He phoned to tell her he would be there in a half hour. Jan said that would be fine. He showered, put on a suit, bought a half dozen red carnations, and went to Aunt Becky's house. In his haste, he shrugged off nagging back pain.

Jan opened the door as he approached and hugged him in the doorway. After entering, he stood back to observe her.

"Beautiful!" he exclaimed. "The most beautiful woman God ever created."

"And happy to have you back – even for a few days," she said wistfully.

He handed her the carnations, saying, "Hurry! We have no time to waste."

Jan picked up her coat and they drove to a restaurant on the west side of town for dinner. Next, they visited Legion Club to dance. She had placed one of the carnations in her hair where it gleamed in the midst of soft waves. Don had forgotten how pleasureful it was to be with Jan, dancing, talking, and laughing.

She learned about his back when they danced. When he seemed to hold back in the Lindy and catchy Latin rhythms, Jan asked if he were in pain. He then explained what had happened, even joked about the lousy parachute-landing fall. She asked if it was serious, whereupon he smiled suggestively and said, "Don't worry, Hon, I can do whatever I want to."

"Well, I certainly hope so!"

Of course, flowers, dinner, dancing, and banter were but preliminaries to what was to happen. In his room at the hotel, they disrobed without rush before lying upon the bed. She sought out the hurtful area on his back and rubbed soothingly. He grimaced at first but gradually relaxed against her. They touched each other, exploring as though everything was new and mysterious. When they sought to join, she gently turned him upon his back and went over him. Placing her hands behind his head, she leaned near and murmured, "Lie still. You must have no pain – only ecstasy."

She moved atop him insistently until he ignored his injury in climax. Jan remained there for the longest time, savoring intimacy to the fullest. Afterwards, when he whispered she meant everything to him, she gave in to her concern.

"Then, how can you leave me?" she asked.

"Please, Jan. Not that. Not now."

Don helped her dress, taking each dainty item from where she had carefully placed it on a chair. He held the dress as she slipped into it and then smoothed the fabric across her taut body. He closed the zipper in back and patted her affectionately as she turned to brushing her hair. Only then did he dress himself.

They visited the Dallas's a couple days later. Her father was disappointed that Don wasn't in uniform but seemed pleased that he had come to say goodbye. Jan and Don let it be known they intended to marry when he returned from Korea. The Dallas's said nothing about Jan's stay in Columbus, or the intimacy Don and their daughter obviously shared now.

Back in Iowa City, Don looked up Bob Gotti. His son's time in the Army had been extended because of the war, but Don Gotti would be returning within a few months to resume boxing. Bob repeated that they expected "to make lotsa money in the pros" over the next few years. Bauer wished them well and departed, with Gotti feinting a blow to Bauer's jaw and saying, "Don't forget to duck this time!"

Jan did not accompany Don to see his family over the weekend because it might be awkward. He swung through Missouri first and looked up Frank and Elsie on a rented farm south of Columbia. His brother and sister-in-law turned thoughtful when Don told them he was on his way to Korea, and they wished him well. Next he drove northwest to Homesite where the rest of the family gathered for Sunday dinner. Don made it a point to talk to everyone that day.

Brad was chagrined. He questioned Don's wisdom in taking ROTC in the first place. "I wouldn't have done that in a million years," he commented.

"It seemed like a good idea at the time," Don replied lamely.

"Well, get out when you can!"

Brad asked about Jan, probably because she hadn't come along.

"She's a bit upset," Don answered, "but actually handling it pretty well. By the way, Brad, I want you to be aware of something."

"Such as?"

"I'm designating you next of kin, so if anything happens take charge. You can handle the folks here, but Jan's different. Her name'll be on my bank account and car title."

"Sure you want to give her that much control?"

"It's part of the bargain," Don explained. "We'll be getting married when I come back, so why not now?"

"See what you mean," Brad replied. "Linda probably would want the same thing. I'll do what you ask, but let's not have any telegrams. O.K.?"

Mom's skepticism ran deeper, however. While they talked in the kitchen, she asked if he and Jan were living in sin. Don parried but couldn't fool Mom. She seemed consoled, however, when Don said they would marry after Korea – probably in the church. Besides, Don and Jan couldn't sin while he was away, could they?

Not surprisingly, she repeated questions first raised when he returned from Europe in 1945."Will you be in danger again?"

"I'll be better off as an officer," he replied.

"And will stress be better, too?"

"Yeah, I'll be busier."

"Have you been to confession lately?"

"It's been a while."

Mom appreciated his honesty. She also understood his reluctance to confess under the circumstances, but leaving Jan would take care of that, wouldn't it?

"Promise you'll go soon," she asked.

"I promise."

Of course, he had never revealed his lapse of faith since Tunisia, but if promising would help her cope, so be it. He didn't discuss Korea with Dad at all. Although Dad suspected something was afoot, he preferred to let things slide on by. Still, Dad's lip quivered when they shook hands; however, Don pretended not to notice.

Deborah was controlled, as always. Paul, too, seemed pragmatic. After all, they had gone through this during World War II, yet life had gone on, hadn't it? Even bad news had softened as grief and sorrow gave way to healing. It was toughest saying goodbye to Jeanne. She cried openly and clutched Don tightly when he hugged her. Verne stood by and merely shook hands, which said it all.

Don kissed Mom goodbye. At a loss for words, he simply said, "Pray for me." She patted his shoulder and said, "I will."

Then he bent down and scratched behind Sparky's ears. "So long, little pal," he said. The nearly blind little pet's tail wagged feebly in farewell.

Don entered his car and drove away, never looking again at those huddled in the Bauer farmyard that Sunday. It was already mid-afternoon and he had another stop to make.

Don Bauer headed straight for Benson, Iowa. He found Speck Mitchell home taking a nap. Speck was surprised, of course, but offered Don a beer. Don turned down the offer, saying he had a long drive ahead to Iowa City.

"I stopped to tell you I'm on my way to Korea," Don announced.

"You didn't get enough fighting last time?"

Don then explained he had taken ROTC to earn a commission in the reserves. Now he had been called up. "So you're right, Speck. I asked for it!"

"Well I'll be damned! You're one of them 'shavetails' now. You know, I always tried to understand you, Don, but never could. Of course, I never understood Duane either."

"I don't know about Duane, but I'm just a slow learner, Speck."

"Yeah, you are, but good luck anyway, you hear? And Don, long as you're there, do me a favor, will ya?"

"If I can."

"Remember how we usta speculate that it ran crossways on Jap women?"

"How could I forget!"

"Well, I never found out cause I went to Europe, so check one out in Japan and let me know, O.K.?"

"Sure thing, Speck. Take care of yourself and I'll see you in a year."

"Hey, I heard that before! Damned if it didn't take over four years to get back last time. Remember?"

"It'll be different this time," Don promised as he departed.

Don and Jan had but five more days together. They had a lawyer draw up power of attorney giving Jan control of his personal affairs. Don added her name to the car title, opened a joint bank account, and said he would send a monthly allotment to cover car payments. Impressed, Jan said she would add to the joint account as well. Clearly, these arrangements were a tangible symbol of their commitments.

Aunt Becky was out of town, so Don was able to move in with Jan those last few days. The night before he departed, she cooked dinner and they shared a bottle of wine. As they lounged later on the sofa, he raised the specter of Rob Stone.

"Will you see him while I'm away?"

"I probably can't avoid it," she replied. "Would you mind?"

After pondering the matter, he answered, "No, but I'll not share you with anyone."

"I know."

"Jan, you must wait for me," he pleaded.

"I will."

"I don't know what brought us together other than Polaris," he reflected, "but it was right that it happened. I've never met anyone quite like you."

He paused, kissed her forehead as she snuggled against him. She took a sip of wine from his glass and handed it back.

"You could find someone better looking," he continued. "You could find someone smarter. You could find someone more amusing. You could find someone with more money. You could find someone who's a better dancer. You could have about anyone you want, I suppose, but you'll never find anyone quite like me. Someone who belongs as I do."

He paused, awaiting her reaction to his little spiel. Jan's reply reminded him that he never really knew what she was thinking.

"This is my fertile time," she said forthrightly.

"So?"

"I want to have your baby."

"Are you serious?"

"Yes."

"But, Jan, we're not married. I'll be gone. You'll be alone." Don spewed out objections as they occurred to him.

"A baby will keep me busy while you're away," she reminded him. "The baby will be *ours*, it will bond us for *all* time."

Jan was right in a way. But he needed time to think and they had precious little time! He took her in his arms, kissed her hair, face and eyes, all the while groping for a reply. Part of her suggestion appealed to him, part of it was anathema. In the end he couldn't accept her proposal.

"I won't put you through having a baby out of wedlock," he argued. "The gossip, the ridicule, the smirks that would plague you. Why, you'd end up hating me!"

"Why should we care what others think?" she asked. "I can handle it. I'm a strong person."

"I know you are, but what you'd be going through would kill me, Jan. I couldn't handle such a distraction in Korea."

That nuance had not occurred to her. The possibility of an adverse impact on him while he was vulnerable gave her pause and she seemed to back off. At least she said no more and went to ready herself for bed.

Through the opened door of the bathroom Don heard familiar sounds of drawers opening and closing, the faucet running, even the brush passing through her hair. Then there was quiet while she took precautions. But he couldn't know what she actually did, of course.

Jan took the pouch from its secluded place, opened it and removed the contraceptive device. She hesitated, pondered her next move. Then half aloud she announced to her image in the mirror, "I, too, must follow Polaris!" She returned the device to its pouch and joined Don lying nude upon the bed.

"Did you say something in there?" he asked.

"None of your business," she quipped.

"Silly girl!"

Don attributed her ardor that night to the occasion. After all, this would be their last lovemaking for a whole year. For a prolonged spell afterwards, she refused to release him, which was all right with Don. When she teased him awake later to make love again, he marveled at her ways of pleasing him. Oh, how he would miss her!

After breakfast the next morning, he donned uniform and packed the bag with his name, rank and serial number stenciled on the side. Jan drove him to Cedar Rapids where he caught a train for Minneapolis. From there he would fly to Seattle.

Jan handled the parting in a manner beyond belief; he was more emotional than she! Whatever had come over her was all right with Don, though; no one wants a scene at the station. "Women puzzle me sometimes," he mused as the train pulled away.

Lieutenant Bauer arrived at Fort Lawton late on February 1st. The next morning he was booked for a flight to Japan as soon as the weather cleared. Heavy fog blanketed McCord Air Force Base for three more days, however. Finally, he and a hundred others boarded a train for Vancouver, B.C., where they caught a chartered Canadian Pacific airliner to Anchorage, Alaska. After refueling, they flew on to Shemya Island in the Aleutian chain for breakfast and another refueling. The replacements arrived at a military base near Tokyo on February 7th and bused onward to Camp Drake.

Although World War II had ended nearly six years earlier, influence of wartime propaganda still perplexed Don Bauer as he observed Japanese on the streets of Tokyo. They seemed as civilized and absent hostility as Americans at this stage. He smiled inwardly when he thought of Speck's curiosity: "We're probably wrong about that, too, old friend!" he mused.

Truth to tell, the Korean Conflict benefited Japan immensely. Vehicles and equipment stockpiled by Americans throughout the Pacific after World War II were now being transshipped to Japan for refurbishing before being sent to Korea. Coincidentally, of course, Japanese industry, obliterated by Allied bombing in World War II, was now being rebuilt with America's help. "Japan, destroyed by war, is being resurrected by war," Don ironically concluded.

While at Camp Drake, replacements again went to firing ranges to familiarize themselves with individual weapons. Some lieutenants, authorized to carry the carbine, preferred the M-1 rifle and were given a choice since the carbine had proved less effective against North Koreans.

Don was inoculated for Plague, a disease carried by rodents that abounded in Korea. He took care of the car-payment allotment and designated Brad as his NOK. Finally, he learned he would end up with the 187th Airborne Regimental Combat Team (RCT). The airborne assignment appealed to him, so he didn't bother calling Colonel Jackson who was commanding a regiment in the 2nd Infantry Division.

Before departing for Korea, Don called Jan. She asked about his back right away and was encouraged when he said the pain was easing somewhat. When she asked if he would fight in the front lines, he diverted by focusing on going airborne where combat roles were different. Then, too, he would draw jump pay, which they could add to their nest egg. She closed by saying she missed him and she loved him. The connection was poor and time limited, but her voice had brought tears to his eyes.

The next morning Don boarded a cargo plane along with other fatigue-clad replacements and crossed the sea of Japan. They passed over Pusan and landed at the airfield near Taegu, site of Eighth Army Headquarters. They were put up in a replacement center and had C-rations for supper. They slept on cots in a tent heated by oil burners. No one complained though, such "comforts" soon would be left behind.

A Liaison Officer from the 187th visited the following day and Don learned he would join 2nd Infantry Battalion's F Company. Captain Roy Bell was the commander and would determine Lieutenant Bauer's exact assignment. Don was certain now that he would end up leading a rifle platoon. When he had a chance, he went to the Red Cross tent and penned a note to Jan, bringing her up to date. He did not elaborate, though.

The wind-swept valley was beastly cold. Replacements were issued parkas with fur-lined hoods so they could cope with the bitter weather. They also received instruction on cold-weather survival, which certainly was timely. Don could well imagine what it must be like in the mountains to the north – worse than Italy!

The 187th RCT had been fighting Chinese around Wonju, but troopers were now returning to home base near Taegu. So Don was delayed until F Company closed in. It was February 17th when finally he climbed aboard a deuce and a half and rode several miles to the 187th bivouac area.

Captain Bell greeted Don warmly and said, "Relax and get acquainted." The troopers would be training and refitting so Bauer would serve as acting exec for the time being. Don realized the temporary job would not only facilitate his meeting people and learning routines but would afford Captain Bell an opportunity to size up his new second lieutenant as well.

As an administrator, Don checked out classified documents first. Sergeant Bailey, Company First Sergeant, opened the field safe and Don found a clutter of SOIs, OP Orders, and unit fund materials. He matched items with the unit log and found everything present. He next identified outdated items for destruction. Then he tidied up the unit fund, which had been neglected since F Company arrived in Korea. Since there had been no expenditures, Don entered deposits and totaled up the balance. Captain Bell was pleased with Don's handiwork. "Next, I want you to help Sergeant Bailey with correspondence," the Captain said.

This didn't set well with Sergeant Bailey, who was responsible for this task. Besides, what did a second lieutenant know about running a company anyway? However, when Captain Bell signed endorsements and letters Bauer prepared, Bailey's attitude changed somewhat. Don knew he had gotten beyond this hurdle when Bailey grumbled, "I can see you've been in the Army for a while."

Two weeks later, Don replaced First Lieutenant Gene Watson as 2nd platoon leader. Watson, who was going on TDY as an air observer, introduced Don to his troopers with the words: "I hope he takes care of you like I did." Don wasn't too surprised at the dig because Watson was reeking of booze at the time.

In a face-to-face briefing, Watson said, "Sergeant Echols is a good platoon sergeant so don't mess him up. Just trust him!" However, when Bauer next talked to Sergeant Echols it was apparent that the Sergeant, too, had been drinking, Obviously, two old troopers had been on a farewell binge and they had questioned qualifications of this novice jumper taking over.

Don recalled that he, too, had been cozy with officers at times in combat, so he decided to overlook this incident. He dismissed Sergeant Echols curtly: "Talking now is waste of time, Sergeant. I'll see you later." Echols got the message, saluted and departed to sleep it off. The following morning, Echols was sober, alert, and courteous.

Don realized he had much to learn—and he still had to prove himself to veteran jumpers. Then there were sensitive things, such as two of his squad leaders were colored. Don had never served with colored soldiers because desegregation came after World War II. But if all colored soldiers were like these two, no adjustment was necessary. Both were proud to be in the elite paratroopers and had already proved their mettle.

Another lesson in leadership came on the third day. Company F made a practice jump on the nearby Naktong River plain. When Captain Bell acted as jump master on Don's C-119, he observed closely so that he could handle veteran jumpers next time. He did lead troopers out the opposite door, however. After landing with just minor aggravation to his back, Don assembled his platoon readily enough. He was holding his own.

Everything now pointed to a combat jump. Troopers did a lot of running, PT, and maintenance. They packed weapons and equipment on pallets for heavy drop. When few complained of the long days,

Don saw this attitude as yet another indicator that combat was just ahead. GIs could always feel it coming.

All doubts disappeared on March 19th when the 187th was sealed into a marshaling area. Briefings began as C-119s and C-46s from all over the Far East began gathering at the airfield. The pace and novelty of this activity tended to alleviate pre-combat stress Don usually experienced. Then, too, other developments served as diversions.

Captain Bell called officers together and pinned silver bars on Don Bauer. He had been promoted to First Lieutenant!

"You're now beyond the idiot stage of being an officer," the Captain said. "Furthermore, you owe us a party when this is over." Lieutenant Bauer had moved another step beyond a novice.

Then there was the untimely letter from Jan Dallas. The first paragraph had the usual things, but the second had a blockbuster!

"*Congratulations!*" she wrote. "*You're going to be a father!*"

It was not just that she had missed her menstrual period, she went on to say, but other telltale signs also indicated pregnancy. However, she would wait until her next cycle passed before seeing a doctor.

"*I hope you are as excited as I am,*" she said in closing.

Don kept the news to himself. At times he was elated and other times upset. She had tricked him! Hadn't they agreed to wait? Was Rob Stone somehow involved? That Don couldn't call or write while they were in the marshaling area frustrated him, too. On the other hand, the delay would enable him to sort things out before confronting Jan. Indeed, Don Bauer was confused at that stage.

Preparing for his first combat jump did take his mind off Jan's surprise somewhat. He sought advice from Sergeant Echols, who had jumped at Sunchon-Sukchon back in October. Echols assured him they were on the right track for this one. "We'll be ready, Lieutenant, no doubt about it!" (Don's prudent handling of the drinking incident was paying off; Sergeant Echols was invaluable.) However, information Lieutenant Bauer received at an officers' briefing gave him concern.

Eighth Army Commander General Matthew Ridgeway wanted to punish overextended enemy forces, improve fighting spirit among his own troops, and regain the initiative on the peninsula. His first step would be Operation Tomahawk, a "hammer-and-anvil" scheme. Tanks would slash through enemy front lines on the Seoul-Kaesong axis as paratroopers dropped near Munsan-ni to cut off an entire North Korean Peoples Army (NKPA) corps. In effect, tanks would "hammer" NKPA against an airborne "anvil," so to speak.

"Overly optimistic," Don thought to himself.

On the night before Tomahawk kicked off, Don lay on his cot unable to sleep. He tried thinking of Jan, but until he talked to her he was stymied. Naturally, his thoughts turned to Tomahawk, which reminded him that by the slimmest of margins he had survived a similar scheme in November 1942.

He was serving with British Commandos in Tunisia at the time. The British First Army Commander sent Commandos on a seaborne raid west of Bizerte. From the beach, they would march cross-country to ambush Germans being driven back by British tanks. The British Commander promised this "hammer-and-anvil" operation would be like shooting fish in a barrel. At the time, Don Bauer actually pitied the unsuspecting enemy.

But planners had not reckoned with difficulties in cross-country marches over Tunisian mountains. Consequently, Commandos arrived at the ambush site behind schedule. Next, British tanks were blasted away, leaving Commandos isolated some twenty-five miles behind enemy lines with no friendly force to rescue them.

Reacting quickly, the Germans smashed the outgunned Commandos with tanks and armored infantry. Survivors scrambled back into the mountains and straggled westward several days without food, rest, or satisfaction before reaching friendly lines. The fish had turned the tables!

Now, on March 22, 1951, Lieutenant Bauer pondered another dimension: Some four thousand American paratroopers would face three to four times that many North Korean fanatics who might surround them in the air head at Munsan-ni. Furthermore, untold thousands of Chinese Communist forces (CCF) were within striking distance as well. Would paratroopers have sufficient ammunition to hold off such hordes?

Don left his warm cot and walked outside the tent into the clear, cold night. He glanced upward and spotted Big Dipper. Then he located Polaris sparkling in the dark heavens.

"North is north, even in Korea," he mused. "Polaris will always be there!"

Troopers were roused at 0400 hours in order to take off three and a half-hours later. They shaved, had breakfast, went to the latrine, and saddled up combat loads: rations, ammunition, weapons, and winter gear. In the first glow of light that morning of March 23rd, paratroopers struggled aboard airplanes at Taegu. Rifle companies would go in first to secure drop zones for heavy drop of artillery and vehicles.

The weather was calm at take off. Lieutenant Bauer, commander of troops on this C-119, was jump master this time. Sergeant Echols sat opposite him near the other exit. In formation, the C-119s headed north on a one-hour flight to Munsan-ni. During the lull, Don's thoughts drifted to Iowa City. It would be about 1700 (5 p.m.) there and Jan Dallas would be back in her room at Aunt Becky's.

"I wonder if Aunt Becky suspects?" Don asked himself. "And Rob Stone? Had Jan told him? Probably. She would seek his support, wouldn't she? And Rob would comfort her! Anything to have Jan back, spend time with her!"

The warning buzzer startled edgy paratroopers. The C-119 was slowing, descending to 800 feet altitude. Bauer and Echols both got to their feet. When Don shouted, "Stand up and hook up!" buckles snapped all along the anchor line cable running throughout the compartment. "Sound off for equipment check;" Lieutenant Bauer called out. The farthest man yelled "Ready!" and poked the man ahead, and he the next, and so on down the line. When Lieutenant Bauer received a poke he assumed all were ready.

Bauer and Echols were at exits, waiting for the pilot to flash green. The lumbering C-119 had slowed perceptibly, but the prop blast still tore at Don's face as he crouched in the doorway. A collective shout rang out when "green" flashed above the door and stick leaders leaped outward, followed by others shuffling forward in noisy cadence.

During descent, troopers called to one another and steered clear to avoid mid-air collisions that could prove fatal if chutes collapsed. Don managed to keep his distance and landed decently and rolled sufficiently to avoid any physical aggravation. On the ground he spotted familiar figures nearby, all abandoning chutes and looking for their leaders.

Bauer headed toward Sergeant Echols. As Don double-timed across the drop zone, he looked about for Captain Bell. In the distance he heard a smattering of small arms fire and intermittent artillery explosions. The enemy was starting to react.

"Any injuries?" Don asked Echols.

"Haven't heard of any, but medics will police 'em up anyway."

"Good! Get the platoon together and follow after me. I'm looking for the Captain."

When he located Captain Bell, Don was told to move his platoon to the woods a couple hundred yards away and prepare to sweep outward. They would be in touch by radio. Don deployed squads as skirmishers and started into brushy area before halting for instructions. Sounds of fighting elsewhere seemed to be subsiding, so maybe the enemy was clearing out. When F Company subsequently swept into the woods for nearly a mile without encountering enemy soldiers, it became clear the NKPA would not contest this drop zone.

Prospects improved further when heavy drop came in on schedule. Soon vehicles and artillery had been recovered and began moving to firing positions. Rifle companies quickly disposed around the drop zone while fuel and ammunition continued to arrive. The "anvil" was in place.

The "hammer" linked up that evening, closing a net that was essentially empty. The NKPA had escaped northward across the Imjin River ahead of the airborne attack; however, opportunity still beckoned.

So abrupt was the NKPA withdrawal that the CCF's right flank was now wide open. Thousands of Chinese remained in position around

Uijongbu and they could be cut off and destroyed —if Americans moved quickly! So General Ridgway sent paratroopers directly eastward across twenty-five miles of hills and mountains to cut enemy escape routes.

Unfortunately for troopers, no trails or roads ran eastward. Therefore, rather than a mad dash, the forced march across streams, obstacles, and mountains occurred at snail's pace. (The trek again reminded Lieutenant Bauer of the Bizerte raid nearly a decade earlier.)

To take his mind off persisting pain in his lower back, Don thought of Jan Dallas. He flip-flopped repeatedly in pondering his dilemma. He was tempted to believe Jan had been with Rob after he left and had become pregnant as a result. The thought infuriated Bauer, caused him to denounce her viciously under his breath. But later he castigated himself for thinking such thoughts. "She wouldn't do that," he reassured himself. "She loves me, only me." If only he could talk to her, hear her reassuring voice.

No enemy activity relieved monotony on this grueling march; however, things did get worse. Whereas they started out in dry weather and on firm soil, a major storm soon developed. Heavy clouds whipped by a brisk wind rolled in at nightfall. A halt was called due to treacherous terrain ahead.

Don surveyed the darkened sky after removing his combat load.

"Even Polaris seems to be deserting me," he mused.

Rain started after midnight, chilling exposed paratroopers. "It's Cassino all over again," Don told Sergeant Echols as they waited beneath a tree for daylight. "At times like this I wonder why I chose Infantry."

"Because we don't know no better, Lieutenant," Echols opined.

Captain Bell briefed platoon leaders before setting out the next morning. Company F would attack part of the battalion objective, Hill 519, which would surely be strongly defended to protect the CCF's retreat from Uijongbu. At the rate of progress to date, and now further slowed by a muddy surface, paratroopers would not reach attack position until late in the day. However with enemy contact growing imminent, patrols were sent to screen the front and flanks on March 26th. The 1st platoon led out, followed by 3rd and 2nd in that order.

Paratroopers slipped and slid forward in a steady downpour all day long without incident. But as darkness settled, 1st platoon drew sniper fire from the front. Lieutenant Brady quickly deployed and sent his troopers up the slope to root out Chinese in outposted positions. The enemy responded with mortar fires, indicating F Company was indeed up against stiff resistance.

Frustrated by the slow pace, and fearful the Chinese would escape entirely, Eighth Army sent tanks careering past Hill 519 to cut roads to the east on March 27th. But rains had softened soil and elevated streams, causing tanks to bog down and become sitting ducks for Chinese anti-tank guns. The futile attempt had to be called off and tanks withdrawn, dashing hopes for a quick success.

Hill 519 must now be taken by infantry supported by artillery. To this end, eight-inch howitzers were added during the night and early on March 28th the UN bombardment started. With shells sailing steadily overhead, paratroopers clawed their way upward against determined defenders.

In a continuing rainstorm, Captain Bell sent 3rd platoon through the 1st at mid-day to freshen the attack. Desperate defenders would not surrender and had to be killed where they stood in foxhole after foxhole. Paratroopers finally occupied the heights by mid-afternoon. However, the Chinese still clung to a spine running eastward.

Captain Bell turned to Lieutenant Bauer and said, "Go get 'em, Don!"

Don studied the narrow approach and then announced, "I'll go straight in with a squad to either side. I'd like artillery to keep their heads down."

"Sure thing, Don."

As Lieutenant Bauer briefed his platoon sergeant and squad leaders, rain slackened and the sun peeped through skittering clouds. Eager NCOs soon led 1st and 3rd squads forward. Don lined up with his radioman and 2nd squad roughly in the middle of the formation. A burst of enemy long-range machine-gun fire buzzed overhead. A round of friendly artillery plummeted into the midst of the enemy position—the registering round! A volley would now follow to cover the platoon assault.

"Let's go!" Don called out as friendly artillery slammed home.

Lead squads jumped up and double-timed forward, shouting and shooting. The enemy shot back with a vengeance. A trooper tossed a grenade to his front. A spurt of enemy machine-gun fire sent dirt and stones flying into Don's legs. A trooper jabbed his bayonet into a foxhole, and then fired a shot. Another hurled a grenade into a bunker. Bauer spotted movement and instinctively sprayed the spot with his carbine. Then all shooting stopped as suddenly as it had begun. A dozen more Chinese soldiers had just died "buying time" for retreating comrades in the valley below.

Don sensed there was more to come, however. "Consolidate!" he ordered as Echols hurried about redistributing ammunition and grenades. Bauer checked squad positions, paying close attention to automatic rifles. Hurry! Hurry! Hurry!

Then the radioman handed Don the walkie-talkie, saying, "It's the Captain."

"They're coming back!" Don blurted into the mouthpiece.

"Are you sure?" a surprised Captain Bell asked.

"There's movement beyond the crest."

"Do you want artillery there?"

"Roger, ASAP!"

Don's troopers were scraping out hollows in the rocky soil, or hopping into foxholes with dead enemy still there. A sniper's bullet whizzed by Don's head and he ducked reflexively. Troopers started shooting back as Chinese approached to buy more time. Friendly artillery hit home, however, scattering the attackers. Troopers cheered.

"That should do it," Don radioed Captain Bell. "Over."

"Roger that. Good work, Lieutenant. Out."

Lieutenant Bauer handed the walkie-talkie back to his radioman and stood up to take another look around. Had he missed anything?

In combat, as in boxing, a man never sees the shot that puts him down – and out! Bright flashes, searing heat and eerie levitation flooded over Lieutenant Bauer on that forlorn Korean mountain in mid-afternoon.

"I'm going down," he sensed. "What's the count? Gotta pick up the count! Back on my feet at eight!"

In this ultimate nightmare, he struggled to get up, to get his feet under him and then hold on, hold on....

The medic, readying a morphine syrette, caught Don Bauer's last words: "Lord, have mercy on me!" The plea was not unusual; indeed, the medic had heard it many times before.

EPILOGUE

Jan Dallas married Rob Stone in May 1951. Indeed, she had gone back to Rob as he had predicted. The marriage caused a stir in the small Iowa town, especially when a baby boy was born to the couple that fall and he was christened Donald B. Stone—the middle name was Bauer.

The following spring, the Rob Stone family moved to Iowa City, where Rob began working as a commercial artist. Jan followed in the steps of Aunt Becky and became a piano teacher in the university music department. She was no longer associated with the Margot Rusel Dance Studio, having set that part of her life aside.

Don Bauer was seldom discussed within the Rob Stone household, but his presence persisted nonetheless. When Jan Dallas would gaze into a clear night's sky, she still asked why her lover had embraced conflict... when he dreaded it so. Polaris, reigning supremely and brilliantly in the northern heavens, was silent, of course. The riddle of Don Bauer remained unsolved – or so it seemed.

Succeeding generations would note that the solution lay within the perspective denied those living at the vortex of the Cold War. The Korean Conflict would end after three torturous years, but contextual hostilities would continue unabated – offering the prospect of more "hot battles" in untold years to come. For those susceptible to the charm of war, peace was nowhere in sight.

Printed in the USA
CPSIA information can be obtained
at www.ICGtesting.com
JSHW082341140824
68134JS00020B/1813